CW01573006

A PROMISE FULFILLED

Eugenie Guest

MINERVA PRESS

LONDON

MONTREUX   LOS ANGELES   SYDNEY

ISBN 1 86106 433 0

First Published 1997 by
MINERVA PRESS
195 Knightsbridge
London SW7 1RE

Printed in Great Britain for Minerva Press

A PROMISE FULFILLED

With many thanks to my friend Jack,
an old soldier, whose narratives of army
life and wartime experiences proved to be of
assistance in the production of this story

Chapter One

The ancient bus came rattling and bumping into the village emitting blue smoke and throwing up a cloud of dust; it spluttered to a standstill in the torrid heat midway down the narrow street. There were only four passengers alighting: two elderly men in worn and dirty working gear; an old woman wearing a long black coat, a shawl around her shoulders, despite the high temperature, carrying a large and apparently heavy basket and last to emerge was the fourth passenger. Neatly dressed, he stood apart from his fellow travellers by the fact that he was some six feet tall, mature and appeared well fed, obviously a visitor from the far away city, or probably from another country. Holding a travel bag in one hand and a suitcase in the other, he stepped down and stood waiting for the bus to pull away, which it finally did with some back firing which left behind a cloud of dust and smoke. Waiting until this settled, he looked around. There was not a soul to be seen, and the only sound to be heard was the barking of a dog in the far distance. Maybe the natives enjoyed a noonday siesta. He remained there for some time, deep in thought, hoping that a human being might appear with whom he could converse, but the street remained empty.

The only two shops to be found among the rows of cottages were a general store and a bakers, both of which were closed. Their grubby appearance and faded adverts, empty shelves and dishes proved them to be poorly stocked. Letting out a deep sigh, he took from his travel bag a map. Carefully studying the page he had turned outwards, yes- this was the village of Mirmskov, or was it? There had not been a name sign as they entered it; he would have to find someone to make sure. Wandering aimlessly along he sensed a familiar feeling. He looked ahead. Ah! yes, the church. There it was - almost at the edge of the village, a grey stone building with a small bell tower at one end of the roof, the heat haze giving it a shimmering aspect, making it look as if the bell in the tower was moving. He made his way towards the church hoping the pastor would be at home, and could give him some of the information he required.

As he drew near to the church he was pleased to see that at least it was open, so taking off his hat he entered enjoying the feeling of cool air faintly scented with incense. He walked down the centre aisle and gazed in awe at the beautiful carvings adorning the ceiling, pulpit and font, the wonder of the stained glass windows, and above all the large silver cross on the altar, at each side of which were the silver candle sticks in view of all.

What a joy to find a corner of the world where lawlessness and desecration of the church had not yet reached. When going to take a seat, in the pew, by which he had put his case he accidentally touched it with his foot; the case fell over making enough noise to startle a bird which had gone to roost in the eaves above. A door at the left hand side of the altar suddenly creaked open, and an elderly grey-haired man appeared. Seeing a stranger sitting in the pew he slowly walked over to him; the man stood up. The priest had to look up to him and addressed him in his own language. Shaking his head the man asked, "Do you speak any English?"

The priest hesitated some moments then answered, "Yes, a little, but I have not used it since the end of the last war." They remained as they were, eyeing each other warily for a few moments, then the priest remarked, "You look tired and are no doubt thirsty. Come into my rooms where we can sit in comfort and I can perhaps get you some refreshments." Picking up his luggage he followed the priest through a door and along a dusty but cool passage, at the end of which another door gave entry into the small but comfortable sitting room of the priest. "Please sit down. I will make you a drink, and perhaps you would like a piece of bread?"

"Thank you, that would be most acceptable," answered the stranger. "I have come a long way and the mode of transport in your country is not the best in the world." He sat down in an old but still comfortable armchair, relaxing whilst the priest busied himself in the tiny kitchen adjacent to the room.

He was soon back carrying a tray which held a jug of milk, a pot of hot coffee, two cups and a plate with two slices of bread and butter. Pouring out the coffee he asked, "Can you drink coffee without sugar? I hope so, as we do not have any at the moment." The man accepted the coffee gratefully, sipping it with some apprehension but, though strong, the milk took away most of the bitter taste. Taking a slice of bread he offered the other to the priest who shook his head. "I have already eaten today. That is for you, please eat you must be hungry." They sat in silence for quite a while, sipping the hot coffee and looking each other up and down. The priest's eyes twinkled with curiosity; it was a rare event to have a visitor to the village, a much rarer one to receive a visit from a foreigner. Breaking the silence at last the priest asked, "Are you an American?"

"No, I am English," he replied.

"So what is an English gentleman doing in this poor isolated part of eastern Europe?" he asked. "Father," he replied, "it is a very long and difficult story which I hope to bring to a satisfactory close and in so doing, your help may be needed. My need at the moment is for somewhere to stay, a bed and meals then perhaps, after resting for a day or two, you will permit me to return and tell you my story, which also divulges my reason for being here, that is of course if you can spare me your time."

"Oh! yes," answered the priest. "I look forward to hearing your story and will gladly help, if it is at all possible. By the way my name is Father Procovitch. What do I call you?"

"My name is Arthur Hallsworth, I come from a small town called Kettering in the English Midlands. Now a widower, my wife died just over two years ago, I am here on a mission, which will be explained to you when next we meet."

Thanking Arthur the priest remarked, "I am trying to think where we can get you a room; there is no hotel in the village and the nearest town is nearly sixty kilometres from here." He sat awhile thinking. Then suddenly his face brightened.

"I wonder," he spoke as if thinking aloud. "Perhaps widow Jaunta would find you a room and meal. She is alone now, her family having left for the city, and her husband died two years ago. If you could pay her a small amount it would be a help to her I am sure, she just about manages to make ends meet. Let us go down and see what can be done." Arthur picked up his case; the priest took the travel bag and going back into the passage they went through a door which led into the village street; the priest led the way, and turning right after passing a few houses they were in the midst of dry and dusty terrain. In the distance, alone in a large plot, some way isolated from the village was a cottage. Pointing in its direction the priest remarked:

"That is the widow's home. Her late husband worked for the owner of a farm nearby, so she will be allowed to remain there for life."

As they neared the building, surrounded by a rough fence, it became apparent that it was well kept. The garden, though dry from shortage of water, still displayed some colour from the fading flowers, and a few hens with their rooster were busy scratching around seeking food. When quite close to the cottage the door leading into the garden opened and a well-built neatly dressed woman of maybe sixty years of age, with greying hair large blue eyes and dark complexion appeared. Smiling, she addressed the priest who, indicating Arthur, started conversation in their own language. Turning to Arthur she indicated they should enter her home; the priest led the way through a long passage. When about halfway he opened a heavy door and went into what seemed to be the living quarters, shabby but spotlessly clean; pointing to the worn old chairs the woman made it clear that they were to be seated. Placing his bags on the floor Arthur sat awaiting the outcome of the lengthy conversation that she and the priest were having.

After some considerable time the priest held up his hand to the woman and, turning to Arthur, informed him, "Widow Jaunta would be delighted to accommodate you; she speaks no English, but I am sure you will not find it very difficult to make your needs known to her. She has little to offer in the way of food at the moment, but you are welcome to share what there is, and you may stay as long as you wish. With the payment she will ask from you for the room and meals, she can replenish her stocks of food and provide you with reasonable fare. She will show you the room when I have gone, as I must leave now to prepare the church for evening Mass, but I doubt if there will be more than six or seven at the service on such a hot evening. Oh! by the way, please address the lady as widow Jaunta we do not often use first names here, I don't even know hers. I have told her your name is Arthur, so that will be the name she calls you by." He rose to leave.

The widow accompanied him to the door where they shook hands and the priest offered a short blessing to her as she bowed her head. When he had left she returned and, with her hands, motioned for Arthur to follow her through a door at the back of the room. They entered a small hallway where, from a row of home-made wooden pegs on the wall, hung several garments for outdoor wear, whilst facing was a short flight of stairs leading to the upper floor. On reaching the small landing off which were two doors the widow opened the one on her right and signed for Arthur to enter. The room contained a large comfortable-looking bed, a dressing table and chest of drawers carved from the solid wood of eastern Europe; in one corner a washhand stand held a large pottery ware bowl and jug. Attached to the side of this was a rail on which the widow placed two towels, and just above hung a small mirror.

Home-made rugs on the floor, wooden pegs fixed on one wall where items of clothing could be hung, and a straight backed chair by the bed all gave the room a homely look. There was a small window to the left of the bed from which flowery curtains were billowing in the light breeze coming from the fields at the rear of the cottage. Glancing round again and then at the widow, who was gazing at him with a look of inquiry in her eyes, Arthur remarked, "Very nice," then, realising that she would not understand he gave the universal sign for okay: 'thumbs up'. Her eyes now alight with pleasure, it was apparent she had been a very pretty woman in her younger years, which showed in her face when she smiled. She let out a sigh, which Arthur took to be relief. Indicating his cases she pointed to the chest of drawers and the pegs. Holding up her ten fingers three times, she made a motion of eating which Arthur took to mean a meal would be ready in thirty minutes; she then pointed to the jug, and made a sign as if pouring water into the bowl. When she had left the room, Arthur found there was a supply of cold water in the jug. Within minutes he was stripped to the waist and washed. Feeling the stubble on his chin he decided also to shave. Hastily unpacking, he donned a clean shirt, combed his silver grey hair and straightened his shoulders.

There was a knock on the door and the widow entered. Arthur pointed to his washing water; the widow lifted the bowl and tipped it out of the open window onto the garden below. She then motioned for Arthur to come downstairs where he found the table was set for two; a patched but clean table cloth, cups, saucers and plates, heavy knives and forks, a small vase of flowers was set in the centre of the table, everything a credit to the lady. She disappeared into the small kitchen beyond the sitting room returning with a large black saucepan, steam rising from the contents; spooning a good helping of the food onto both plates she replaced the saucepan and brought forth a bread basket containing some crusty rolls. Although very hungry Arthur sat gazing at the food, it seemed appetising enough, he could see potatoes, carrots and what appeared to be swede or turnip, and chunks of meat in thick gravy. Looking at him she indicated he should eat, so Arthur tucked in. It was surprisingly tasty and he wondered what the meat was; the widow must have guessed his thoughts. Speaking his name rather indistinctly she made some movements with her hands which gave him to realise they were eating either rabbit or hare. The meal over, she cleared away the dishes, and came back with a pot of hot coffee and a jug of milk but no sugar. Arthur drank the unsweetened coffee handed to him, then went to sit in the easy chair to which the widow pointed whilst she went back into the kitchen.

Arthur could hear her washing and wiping the dishes, after which she came out carrying a pot containing the vegetable peelings and other bits and pieces. Going into the front garden the hens and rooster came dashing towards her as she scattered the food on the ground for them; she then went to the back of the cottage and into the hen house, returning with four large new laid eggs. By this time Arthur was yawning, and doing his best to keep awake. The clock noisily ticking away on the shelf above the fire place pointed to eight o'clock; Arthur consulted his own watch which showed it was just after eight. The widow sat down facing him, and in sign language gave him to understand that he could retire to his bed whenever he liked to do so. Feeling it would be ill mannered to retire so early he stood up and, looking through the window, pointed to the back garden. Understanding his meaning, she led him round the side of the cottage and there to Arthur's surprise he found the rear garden – a picture to behold. Vegetables of all description were growing in well-ordered rows with not a weed in sight, surrounding flower beds were a riot of colour, the whole carefully tended and well watered. "You do all this alone?" Arthur signalled; nodding assent she led him to the hen roost at the far side of which was a large compost heap, and leaning nearby were the old tools she apparently used.

Lifting one, Arthur found it rough and heavy but clean and sharp. It was obvious the woman was hard working and endeavouring to be self sufficient; the cottage was scrupulously clean and neat and although her clothes were worn and patched they too were clean and tidy; she was trying to make the best of what little she had, and live a decent life. Arthur then remembered that he had not sorted out with her what payment to make during his stay; finding a scrap of paper in his pocket he wrote down a sum of money in their currency which he then handed to the widow indicating the days Sunday to Sunday in his diary. Looking at the sum and the days her face beamed, she looked more closely then shaking her head took his pen and, crossing off the original sum, halved it. Arthur shook his head, "No". He rewrote the first offer, nodding in the affirmative. The widow seemed unsure but, after a while, accepted it and they returned indoors. The time was now well over nine o'clock so, making his way towards the stairs, Arthur bowed to her saying good night. She answered in her own language. He went to his room, undressed and slid into the rough but cool sheets and was dropping off to sleep when he heard her come up the stairs, and enter her own bedroom. Arthur fell into a deep sleep, awaking only once in the night; the air was cool and clean with a silence so deep as to be almost heard, and sleep took over once more.

When he finally emerged it was to find the sun streaming through the open window and a fresh breeze gently wafting the curtains. Picking up his watch from the bedside chair on which he had placed it last night, he was amazed to see the time was nearly nine thirty a.m. Going over to the bowl, he found the jug almost full of fresh water. He hastily washed and dressed and went down to the living room. Coming in from the front garden, widow Jaunta wished him a cheery good morning in her own language then clasping her hands together she laid her cheek on them as if asking, "Had he slept well?" Arthur smiled and nodded. Going into the kitchen she came back shortly with a plate of bread and butter, two boiled eggs, the pot of hot coffee and jug of milk, but no sugar. These were placed on the table and she indicated for him to eat. He made short work of his meagre but satisfying breakfast. Waiting until he had finished, the widow produced a crumpled piece of paper from her apron pocket and handed it to Arthur. Carefully unfolding it he found written in barely legible English a note from the priest saying, "Please come to my home tomorrow, Thursday at ten a.m., when perhaps you will be able to tell me the reason for your visit to our impoverished little village. I am most interested, and hope I may be able to help you solve your apparent quest in our country."

He remained seated at the table for some moments, during which time the widow went back into the kitchen emerging with a basket of washing on the top of which lay the shirt, socks and underwear Arthur had discarded when retiring last night and placed on the chair at his bedside. The dear woman must have taken and washed them long before he had awakened. Rising from his chair he went to stand by the window, and watched her pegging the washing on the line. He noticed the old fashioned pegs so like the ones used many years ago by his mother, made from split willow bound near the top with a band of tin and bought at the door from a gypsy. Turning away he began by clearing the breakfast table, taking the things into the kitchen, where in one corner he saw a brightly burning stove on the top of which was a large black kettle full of hot water. Finding an enamel bowl in the worn old sink, he poured some of the heated water into it and started to wash up the items they had both used. Beside the sink was a bucket into which egg shells and edible bits were put, presumably to help feed the chickens. Carefully putting his own scraps among them he carried on with his self-appointed chore. He sensed the presence of the woman behind him and, turning round with a cup in his hand, saw a look of amazement on her face. Bursting out crying, she rushed into the garden, wiping away the tears with her apron.

Arthur was somewhat perplexed, not knowing what he had done to upset her. Completing his task he wiped his hands dry on the rough towel hanging by the kitchen sink. He went to the living room window and saw the widow readjusting some of the clothes on the line. Looking at the clock on the shelf, he checked his own watch with it and realised it was time to be setting off for the church, and his appointment with the priest. Putting on a lightweight jacket and a hat, he went in to the garden. Going up to the widow he pointed to the distant church and the note in his hand. Nodding that she understood, she in turn held up six fingers and made a motion of eating, indicating that a meal would be ready for six o'clock in the evening. Making his way onto the road he walked towards the church in leisurely fashion, trying to puzzle out in his mind what had caused the widow to burst into tears. He had not reached a decision by the time he arrived at the side door of the church which led into the priest's living quarters. Arthur's knock was quickly answered; the door creaked open to reveal the elderly priest in his long black robe smiling, and saying:

"Please come in. I am sure between us we have much to talk about." As they entered the sitting room Arthur took off his hat and jacket, and sat in the same easy chair he had previously occupied.

The priest, having gone into the kitchen, now returned with a tray on which was a pot of coffee and two cups. Milk and sugar were apparently not available.

"First let us take a cup of coffee, then you can begin your story." As they sipped the hot black coffee, Arthur thought again of the widow's tears and decided to ask the priest if he could explain the reason for them, telling him how he had cleared the breakfast table, and was at the sink in process of washing up the crockery when the widow walked in, and seeing Arthur doing this chore, she had burst into tears and rushed outside. Father Procovitch smiled saying, "I think that was the only household chore, that her late husband ever did in the cottage. Seeing you do the same one must have brought back memories of him. They were a devoted couple, and lived in harmony with hardly ever the sound of a cross word between them. He worked hard to provide for her and the family, two sons and a daughter. The elder son died just before the war ended. The other son is married but lives and works in the city; her daughter is married but has no children. She and her husband live in a small town some 100 kilometres from here; they both visit once or twice each year, and she goes to stay with one or the other at Christmas time. I feel sure that, could she speak English, the explanation given for her tears would have been memories of her late husband doing his daily chore. How are you getting on with her, do you have difficulty understanding each other?"

Arthur replied, "No, with a few hand signs, a nod, or a shake of the head we manage quite well. I hope to learn a little of your language in time, and so make myself better understood eventually."

They sat for a while slowly drinking the last of the coffee, when Father Procovitch remarked, "I am now ready to hear your story, and why you feel that perhaps I can be of help. I am a good listener, so take your time. Should there be anything I do not understand, may I stop you for an explanation?" Leaning back in his chair, making himself more comfortable, Arthur replied:

"Yes certainly."

'Now where do I start?' He thought for a short time, then taking a deep breath, started to unfold his reason for visiting this impoverished village, seemingly at the back of beyond. "I think it will be best, Father, if I start at the beginning."

Chapter Two

"A year before the last war broke out, nearing the age of eighteen, I joined the local Territorial Army, at that time part of the Northamptonshire Yeomanry Regiment. I was also a member of the Rover Scout group in Kettering, my birth place. Although our people were hoping war could be avoided, it seemed apparent that it was imminent. I knew that if our country should be involved I would be called up for service in the armed forces eventually, so decided that some previous military training would be an advantage for when that day arrived. As you are well aware, England declared war on Germany, and at the age of twenty I was called up for military service and drafted into the Northamptonshire Regiment of Infantry. After a short period of training we were sent to France as part of the British expeditionary force. What a debacle that proved to be, our troops being forced to leave France via Dunkirk, resulting in a massive loss in men and weapons. After a short rest at an army barracks in the south of England, our regiment was reformed with many new recruits, which necessitated fresh training. We were then transferred to a camp near Southampton and supplied with kits suitable only for a hot climate, cotton shirts, shorts, socks, etc. Southampton docks was our next stop to embark on the troop ships awaiting us. During our passage out which took several weeks, we encountered some hair-raising moments, one being when a troop ship was sunk by enemy submarine, resulting in heavy loss of lives.

"On arrival at Port Alexandria we joined the Eighth Army. Our regiment, the Desert Rats, took part in many of the battles fought back and forth in the Middle East until we defeated Field Marshall Rommel. During one of the battles I sustained a shrapnel wound in the chest and was sent back to the field dressing station for medical attention. At that time I was a sergeant but on returning to my regiment I was informed of my promotion to Company Sergeant Major. This came as a pleasant surprise which I gladly accepted, as it not only gave me more responsibility but also a rise in pay.

"Some months after hostilities ended in the Middle East, we received orders to leave for another war zone. After being at sea for some days news came through that we were going to the Far East, Thailand, the Philippines, or some other God-forsaken place no one had ever heard of. Our journey was to take us via Darwin, Australia. This pleased us all as it meant we would have a week or two on dry land before going into battle again. However, that was not to be. Within 200 miles of Darwin our convoy was turned round and sent to Hong Kong where we disembarked and proceeded up the Peninsula to try to stop the Japanese army who were making a very heavy push, in an effort to take Singapore. The pressure was far too great for us to stop them, so we made an orderly retreat back into the city. Within days the Japanese were at the gates of the city. High Command then decided to get out, with as much of our arms and equipment as it was possible to save.

"I, and what was left of our regiment, embarked on the last but one Troop Ship to leave Singapore harbour with our enemy only a few hundred yards away. We struggled aboard leaving behind many dead and wounded. No one had any idea where we were going until several days later, when we learned that our destination was England, where we would refit and, with an intake of new recruits, get our regiment back to strength. After a long and hazardous journey with little food, the liner was well overloaded with men. On arrival at Portsmouth harbour, we disembarked and were sent to camp in tents near Weymouth to recuperate."

The priest stirred, making himself more comfortable in his chair. Arthur paused, saying, "I do hope I am not boring you with my story?"

"No, no!" exclaimed Father Procovitch. "Please continue, I find it most fascinating. You must have had a most exciting time in your youthful years. Please continue."

Arthur settled back and picked up the thread of his story again.

"Our training began all over again and from the start day by day it became apparent that this was for something big and of significant importance. We were granted a week's leave. I went home to see my parents and enjoyed the trip back to civvy street, calling in at the local pub and club for a beer when available. I also visited relatives many of whom I had not seen for years. My parents were coping well under wartime conditions, being delighted with the extra rations I had been able to provide.

"During that week rumours were being spread of the possibility of an impending invasion of France. It was then I realised that all the special training we were having was towards this end. My family bade me a tearful farewell and a few days after returning to my regiment we were all confined to barracks, where everything was tightly closed. No letters were allowed to be written home, civilians were all evacuated from the area, and our training continued whilst we awaited the signal for the expected invasion to take place. It was like being in a vast prison camp. Rumours flew around and everyone talked only of where we might land, and what it would be like. We moved out of camp in the very early hours of June 6th, arriving at Weymouth harbour to board the Liberty Ships of the American navy and set off across the Channel for an unknown destination. The sun was rising as we neared the Normandy coast, to see what must have been the greatest armada of Battle Ships ever, throwing everything they had carried onto the beaches and dunes beyond. Our ship got as near to the beach as was possible without being grounded on the sea bed; we scrambled down the nettings into the landing barges, struggling ashore under heavy fire with the American infantry alongside taking cover in the dunes, as speedily as we could. From then on it was hard fighting through France to the Falais Gap, where we sustained a heavy loss in men. On into Belgium then Holland, where we were withdrawn from the front line, to re-equip and re-enforce our Companies, in preparation for the battle for the Rhine crossing and on into Germany. Once again the infantry took the brunt of the advance with the inevitable heavy loss of lives.

"Many of the new replacements were of other nationalities: Poles, Ukrainians, Lithuanians and some from your own country, they had escaped the German occupation in the early part of the war and fled to England. It was there that I met one of your fellow countrymen, Sergeant Ivor Kaldev. He was a very brave and resourceful soldier, who spoke some English; fighting alongside each other in that terrible battle, we became firm friends. It was soon after crossing into Germany that Ivor saved my life. We had just dug in on the bank of the river, with the enemy only a few hundred yards from our positions, when a German hand grenade landed close to our dug out. Without a moment's hesitation Ivor grasped the handle, intending to throw it back towards the enemy, when it exploded taking off Ivor's right arm and causing a terrible wound in his side. Whilst calling for a medic, I did all in my power to staunch the flow of blood, but I knew in my heart that Ivor could not make it, so I made him as comfortable as was possible. Looking beseechingly at me Ivor pulled from his battledress pocket some papers which he held out to me. Gasping for breath and trying to make his voice heard above the din of battle, he thrust the papers into my hand saying:

'Here is the address of my home. As far as I know, my mother and sister are all that is left of my family. I have been unable to contact them since I escaped from the German army in 1940.' Becoming silent for a moment, and grasping my hand he pleaded:

'If and when you can, Arthur, please go and find them, if they are alive, and tell them of me.' I held his hand a moment more and promised I would do this for him. Ivor died there in the mud, beside the river Rhine.

The battle raging around us seemed to have reached an even higher level, when above the crack of small arms, and the thumps of the heavy artillery from the other side of the river, I heard the commander's whistle. This meant we were to advance and try to take the forward positions of the enemy, now decimating the boats carrying the reinforcements over the river. It was with a heavy heart at the loss of a good friend that I had to leave Ivor's body lying there. Had he not grabbed the hand grenade and moved out of the trench I too would have probably been lying there, seriously injured or dead beside him. There was no time for recriminations and tears. I thrust the papers he had given me into my pocket and fought on alongside my company. Soon afterward I was promoted to the rank of Regimental Sergeant Major.

"We at last reached Hamburg where, on Lunenburg Heath the German army surrendered to Field Marshall Montgomery, and we were at last able to rest a while, although the war still continued in the Far East against the Japanese."

Arthur lapsed into silence rose from his chair and stretched. Father Procovitch also stirred. He looked up at Arthur saying, "Perhaps you have talked long enough for today. We could continue some other time, I shall be free most of Saturday."

Glancing at his watch Arthur saw it was well past two o'clock. The priest also looked at the time. "Good gracious," he exclaimed, "you must be thirsty and hungry." Rising from his chair he hurried into the tiny kitchen. Arthur also rose and, stretching his arms above his head took a deep breath. Slowly exhaling he walked about the room, reliving memories in his mind, causing sighs and frowns for a moment or two. He was still standing when the priest returned with a tray on which was a jug of clear water, two glasses and two plates of bread and cheese. "I am sorry, there is only goats cheese. I hope you can eat it. We have few milking cattle in this area, but goats seem to live on anything. The water is cool and pure drawn from our own well. It is said to have medicinal properties. Perhaps that is why, at the great age of seventy-eight years I am still active and fairly fit," he laughed.

Arthur took the proffered glass of water, and the slice of bread and cheese. Sitting down, he proceeded to refresh himself. The cool water had a similar taste to some he had tried in one of the German spas at which he had been stationed for a short time after the ending of the war; the bread and cheese tasted good. The priest made short work of his own repast, then, turning to Arthur remarked, "If you feel you have talked long enough today, leave the rest and resume on Saturday." Draining the last drop of water from his glass Arthur replied:

"I trust you are not unduly tired with the episode of my life so far. I will add a piece to bring this more up to date and will then do as you say, and continue on Saturday. I must soon return to widow Jaunta's as she indicated the meal would be ready by six o'clock, but before then, I am sure there will be some little jobs I can do to help her with the household chores. She is a very hard working woman and deserves a little help, that is, if she will allow me to help." The priest laughed saying:

"She is a very independent person but I'm sure she would not refuse your help with any of the heavy jobs, so continue Arthur, then I can prepare for evening Mass. The weather is getting cooler. It is possible we shall have a storm before long. It has been some weeks since we had any rain to speak of, that is why the crops are not doing so well, with the ground so dry. But enough of our problems, please go on."

Once more collecting his thoughts together Arthur returned to his story.

"Well, Father it was then I found the time to really look at the papers which Ivor had handed to me before he died. I had previously glanced at them, but had little time to read them properly. His birth certificate, nationality papers with his home address and next of kin. He had been doing national service in the army here for a year. There were official papers giving details of his entry into Great Britain as a refugee and the certificate giving the date of enlistment into the British army, British army papers and pay book which put his age at the time of his death, to be just over thirty years. Included was also a very faded and crumpled photograph of an elderly lady and a young girl of about sixteen or seventeen years of age holding hands. This appears from the background to have been taken outside a cottage very similar to that of the widow Jaunta's.

"Written on the back is something in your language, which might be the names of his mother and sister, if it is them pictured on the photo, and the date is May 23rd 1935. By this time, our regiment had split up, and I realised that the few soldiers who came from your country to serve with distinction in the British army had already been repatriated to their homes. There being no one at hand I could ask to translate the documents or photo, I carefully placed them in a strong envelope well sealed and sent them to my parents, to be kept in a safe place until the end of hostilities, when I hoped to return home safely myself. I was feeling a little apprehensive that I might be sent to the Far East to help the rest of our Brigade finish the war out there, but after the two atom bombs were dropped on Japan the Japanese decided to surrender to General McArthur, thus ending World War Two. With the ending of hostilities, I was granted two weeks end of war leave, during which time I met an attractive young lady employed in a shop near my home. We enjoyed each other's company, and spent quite some time together during that fortnight. I then had to return to Barracks; having served throughout the war I was in the first batch to receive demob papers. After being fitted out with civilian clothing, I promptly went back home, where a most pleasant surprise awaited me; the young lady of my previous acquaintance had made friends with my parents and was there with them at my home, waiting to welcome me back to civilian life once more.

"After courting for some time and being very much in love with each other we decided on the date for our wedding and were married in May 1946, but sadly did not have any children. In those days the cause of infertility was unknown to medical science. Nevertheless we were very happy; my wife's sister, living close by, had a boy and a girl who visited us several times a week so, though we had no family of our own, we were privileged to share the love and affection of those two, enjoying the fun and games of their childhood. Christmas and birthdays being highlights of the passing years, when presents were given and received, their love and devotion as age crept on repaid us tenfold. I had a safe responsible position at a cereal manufacturing company in a nearby town, thus enabling us eventually to purchase our own home, and enjoy life more fully. My retirement at the age of sixty-five was marred by the death of my mother closely followed by my father. Clearing out their home, I found locked away in Dad's bureau the papers Ivor had entrusted to me. I was filled with remorse at my forgetfulness. These I carefully removed to put safely away in my own home, hoping that somehow soon I might be able to carry out Ivor's wishes."

Glancing at his watch Arthur saw it was nearing four o'clock. "It is time for me to be returning to widow Jaunta's," he remarked. The priest also rose from his chair saying:

"Yes, my Son, I also have one or two things to attend to. Your story is very intriguing. I look forward to hearing more of it on Saturday. If you have them with you, please bring Ivor's papers. I can at least translate their meaning for you."

"They are in a briefcase, safely locked away in my suitcase. Had I thought of it, I could have brought them with me today," remarked Arthur. The priest led the way to the outer door, on the opening of which they were both surprised to feel a strong cold wind blowing with dark thundery clouds looming up on the horizon. Looking at them with a certain amount of alarm showing on his face the priest held out his hand, saying:

"Oh dear, it looks as if we are going to have one of our heavy storms within the next hour or so. It is quite common for this part of the country to suffer a period of heavy rain after a long dry spell such as we have just had. The rain will be most welcome, but storms are often the cause of heavy damage. You had better make haste and try to get to the cottage before the storm breaks."

Putting on his jacket and hat, Arthur shook hands with the priest and stepped out briskly to walk home. As he neared the gate the first spots of rain were falling onto the dry dusty road leaving small circles where they hit the ground. The widow stood in the front garden, having just finished feeding the hens. She looked up as Arthur came through the gate. Carefully closing it behind him he waved, and reaching her took the old bucket from her. She pointed up toward the sky and Arthur guessed she was indicating the storm.

By this time the wind had become much stronger, and the dust not yet dampened by the rain was blowing about like miniature sand storms. They made for the front door of the cottage together as the rain suddenly increased in volume. As the widow closed the door, a flash of lightning lit the interior followed almost immediately by a loud clap of thunder which shook the cottage, then came the heavy rain battering the roof and beating on the windows. As he removed his jacket and hat Arthur noticed a side section of one of the front windows was slightly open, so he walked over to close it before the rain came in. The widow went into the kitchen to prepare the evening meal. As the storm increased its velocity, flashes of lightning illuminated the shabby but clean room, whilst each clap of thunder seemed to shake the cottage to its foundation. Arthur decided to go to his room and change into something more comfortable than the suit he was wearing. On entering his room he noticed the mat near his bed was wet and a steady drip of water was coming from the ceiling. Quickly reaching for the wash basin he placed it under the leak. "There must be a loose slate on the roof," he thought. "Perhaps when the storm is over I can refix it that is, if a ladder long enough for me to reach it can be found."

Returning downstairs he found the widow laying the table for the evening meal. Seeing him she spoke his name and pointed to the chair set at the table, then went back to the kitchen to return with, in one hand a delicious-looking pie, in the other a dish of fluffy mashed potatoes. Cutting the pie in two she placed a piece on each plate. Handing him the dish of potatoes, the remainder of which she put on her own plate, the pie lived up to its first appearance, the crust being fairy light and the filling delicious. They ate in silence for outside the storm still raged, making all but hand sign language impossible. When the meal was finished, she rose to clear the table; placing his hand gently on her arm, Arthur shook his head and pointing to the armchair said, "Sit down and rest." She understood his meaning and sat down. Arthur cleared the table and did the washing up. When he returned the widow was fast asleep despite the raging wind, creaking doors and windows and the loud claps of thunder; resting back in the chair completely relaxed in sleep the lines and wrinkles were partly smoothed away from her features. Gazing at her for a few moments he realised how exhausted she must be from her many chores. He went quietly to his room to find the bowl almost full from the leaking roof. He emptied it out of the window and replaced it under the dripping spot. Taking from his case the book he had been reading during his journey here he returned downstairs to find the widow still sleeping; the darkness was rapidly approaching, so with a match he found on the mantel shelf he lit the oil lamp, and settled down to read.

Chapter Three

The storm seemed to have abated, the thunder receding into the distance, when the widow suddenly awoke and, looking startled, sat rubbing her eyes. She glanced at the clock and seeing it was nearly nine o'clock jumped up from her chair looking rather embarrassed. She rushed into the kitchen and came back holding out to Arthur the clothes she had washed for him. Everything was freshly ironed. Taking them, his "Thank you they look lovely," must have been understood by the widow for a slight blush appeared on her face as she turned to go back into the kitchen. Taking the clothes to his own room he carefully placed them on a shelf in the cupboard and emptied the bowl again, although there was not so much water in it this time. Returning to the downstairs room he found a jug of hot coffee had been prepared. They sat in silence sipping their drink and looking across the table at each other. Conversation was impossible until they had learned a little of each other's language. Then Arthur thought of an idea which might help. Placing the book he had been reading near to the widow he pointed to it saying "book". She looked rather puzzled so he repeated, "book...book". It then dawned on her that he was telling her what it was called in English. After several attempts she made a sound which was near enough to be recognised. She then exchanged the word for "book" in her language. It soon became quite a game. The widow was intelligent and quick to learn. Arthur too soon picked up the pronunciation of words in her language. Thus they continued with "chair", "sit", as Arthur sat down, "table", "room", "window", "clock", "shirt", "shoes", "socks", and so on.

It was well past eleven o'clock when they noticed that the storm had passed. The room was hot and stuffy so, as the rain was over the windows were opened wide and a cool clean breeze wafted through the room. They sat for a short time then the widow indicated that she was retiring to her bed. Arthur remained to finish the last part of the chapter of the book he was reading then, taking the candlestick from the table, lit the candle, put out the lamp and he also retired. There was still a few inches of water in the bowl on the floor of his room, so he placed it on the table to use for washing in the morning. Making a mental note that he would try and fix the leak next day, he got into bed and was soon asleep; he awoke with the sun streaming into his room and the cool breeze coming in through his partly open window gave a fresh clean smell. His watch showed the time to be just after eight o'clock. He hurriedly washed and shaved in the bowl of rain water, then poured it out of the window, and dressing himself in a check shirt and jeans he slipped his feet into a pair of shoes and ran downstairs to find the widow about to start her breakfast. She smiled and went into the kitchen, returning with two boiled eggs and a plate of bread and butter; the coffee pot was already on the table. Arthur filled his mug, and they sat and enjoyed breakfast together. Getting up from the table, both of them were intent on clearing the table but the widow, to his surprise, indicated the chair, saying "sit", her first attempt at English and, gathering up the dishes took them to the kitchen where he heard her washing them.

He rose and went to look out of the window. The hens in the front garden were scratching away with renewed energy finding worms that had come to the surface after the rain, the ground now well watered looked fresh, the flowers clean and bright. He remembered the leak in the roof and going into the kitchen, took the widow by the hand and led her up to his room. Entering, he beckoned her in. She hesitated at the door with a puzzled look on her face. 'Oh!' thought Arthur, 'I hope she does not think I desire to take an unfair advantage of her.' For a moment he watched her standing by the door, not sure whether or not to enter. He pointed to the wet patch on the ceiling, then to the mat on the floor, picked up the bowl and, placing it over the wet patch, lifted it and going to the window, made it appear as if he were pouring water away, she let out a sigh, which to Arthur sounded like relief. A smile lit up her face and she burst into a peal of laughter, and there was evident in her eyes a twinkle of interest in him that Arthur failed to notice. They went downstairs and outside to view the roof. Yes, a loose slate was laying sideways from the others. He pointed to the slate and then made a climbing motion. She understood a ladder was needed, and shook her head. 'Perhaps there is some one in the village from whom we could borrow one,' he thought. I must ask the priest if he knows of anyone who might have one to loan us.

He stood, breathing in the cool fresh air. The widow had gone to the back of the cottage, from where he now heard the sound of sawing.

Going to the rear he found her trying to saw through large thick pieces of wood which he guessed were to be fuel for the cooking stove. Making a chopping sign he asked, "Have you an axe?" She nodded and opened a small door at the side of the chicken house, reached in and handed him a large heavy axe. It was blunt and rusty. He rummaged around in the shed, until he found a sharpening stone, and seating himself on an upturned log he wet the stone in a nearby pool left by the storm, and proceeded to sharpen the axe. The widow watched silently for some time then disappeared into the cottage. After testing the axe a few times, Arthur was satisfied with the sharp edge, and began to cut the wood into pieces suitable for the stove. Warming up to his work he slipped out of his shirt. Unbeknown to him the widow was watching him from the rear window, and from the look on her face she was admiring his strong brown arms and firm manly torso. Letting out a quiet sigh of pleasure she turned away, perhaps ashamed of her thoughts and the emotion they aroused. Arthur was busy enjoying the exercise when he heard voices at the front. He carefully laid down the axe, remembering what he had learnt as a Rover Scout never to leave an axe blade exposed, and putting on his shirt he went round to the front garden, where the priest was talking to the widow.

"Oh! there you are," he exclaimed. "I wondered how you both fared during the storm." Pointing to the loose slate on the roof Arthur asked if there was anyone in the village who had a ladder.

"Leave that to me I will get someone to come and fix that."

"I came to suggest an outing for you. Today there is a market held in the town a few kilometres from here, and I thought you might like to take widow Jaunta to do some shopping this afternoon. I'm sure she needs to replenish her stocks. You may also require some goods. You will find a bank there if you should need to exchange English money to our currency. It would do her a power of good to get out for a while. You might also enjoy the change, the old bus on which you arrived leaves the main street at about one o'clock; it leaves town for the return journey at five o'clock taking about half an hour each way."

He then turned to speak to the widow. Making a guess that he was telling her of his proposal, Arthur nodded his head saying, "Sure I would love to take a trip out. I need to change some travellers' cheques and there are a few items I could do with."

The widow's face lit up with undoubted pleasure, and saying something to the priest she hurried indoors and went to her room to change, ready for the outing. Arthur shook hands with the priest, thanking him for the kind suggestion, and as he turned to leave, reminded him of their meeting arranged for the next day. Going to his room, he hastily freshened up and changed into a clean shirt and light suit, returning downstairs he found the widow waiting neatly dressed in a pretty floral two-piece suit and straw hat, a large wicker basket on her arm, and a well worn leather hand bag suspended from her hand.

She pointed to the clock which showed a quarter to one. Arthur put on his hat and followed her out of the cottage, ensuring that his wallet was safely inside his jacket pocket; they walked down to the village street arriving at the bus stop at the same time as the noisy creaking old bus. Arthur helped the widow onto the bus, then went aboard himself and they sat down side by side, to the amazed and curious gaze of the other passengers.

Thus started their journey to the market town. The widow turned to Arthur with a smile of delight on her face, slipped her arm into his and settled down to enjoy her outing. Gazing down at her, he saw not only her gentle smile but an expression of infinite pleasure, and felt slightly but pleasantly surprised when she placed her arm through his. He looked round at the other passengers on this dilapidated mode of transport, a mixture of men and women, the men mainly attired in clean collarless shirts and old but tidy suits, the women (with the exception of two young-looking ones), dressed in long coarse-looking black dresses with a shawl over their shoulders. The two younger ones wore flowery printed summer dresses, and laughed and chatted away all through the journey, in contrast to the older people who sat in passive silence all the way to the town.

Arthur took stock of the countryside as they went along, and it appeared that most of the fields were set with corn or root crops, although some had mounded up rows of potatoes. There were not many trees and few bushes to be seen, giving a rather barren look to the area. The widow sat with her eyes closed as if she were asleep. She stirred to make herself more comfortable, but did not release her arm from beneath his, which made Arthur feel that perhaps she was just relaxing. The journey proved rather bumpy as the roads were not very well maintained but, after a while, (it seemed to be in the middle of nowhere), the bus came to a stop to pick up three more passengers. Looking around, there was not a house, or sign of habitation anywhere so Arthur surmised that these people must have walked from farms a considerable distance away to reach the road. The bus chugged slowly along, blowing exhaust fumes from the rear, causing a cloud of dust to follow in their wake. Arthur was about to close his eyes against the glare of the sun, when the bus turned onto a metalled road in much better condition than the one on which they had previously travelled. As the driver picked up speed, he saw traffic going by in the opposite direction – vintage cars, farm carts and tractors. Now and then a car would overtake them, going he supposed to the town for which they were heading. The widow suddenly sat up, turned to Arthur and spoke rapidly. Realising that he did not understand, she pointed to the front of the bus then to her basket, and held up the fingers of her hand twice.

'Oh! yes,' thought Arthur, 'ten minutes and we reach the town.' Nodding to her she again smiled, which gave her a homely pleasant and friendly appearance, he decided.

The traffic built up, and buildings were to be seen in the distance; streets with houses on either side, and children playing on the sidewalks appeared, even a grass-covered park with a play area. Most of the houses looked dingy, some very much in need of a coat of paint. It seemed a fairly large town, the tall black chimneys seen in the far distance were probably, thought Arthur, the sign of some sort of industry. Glancing at his watch he found the bus was running late, as it was now 1.45 p.m. The interior of the bus was hot and stuffy with an overpowering smell of body sweat from the passengers, so he was hoping there might be a bar near the bus stop where he could quench his thirst, and hopefully find a toilet. Perhaps the widow would also like something cool – he had no idea whether she liked strong drink, but at least they could have a lemonade or a coca cola, if such commodities had yet reached this outpost of civilisation. They turned a corner and the bus shuddered to a stop. To the left of the bus was the large area of market stalls the people busily making their purchases, to the right hand side was a row of shops which also appeared to be doing a brisk trade, if the number of people going in and out was anything to go by. The passengers started to pick up their baskets and leather bags then began to alight, stepping out into the heat of the sun.

Jumping down, Arthur helped the widow down to the pavement. He searched around, hoping to find a bar. When she looked at him he made a sign as if drinking; nodding she took his arm and, avoiding the traffic, led him across the road into a small lane between the shops, at the end of which was the hostelry he had been hoping to find. It was crowded, mostly with men drinking a brew which looked like dark beer. Without pausing for breath she pushed her way up to the bar with him. The man serving behind it turned to look at her; his face lit up with pleasure and, without more ado, he pulled a large glass of beer from the tap and handed it to the widow. They immediately launched into a babble of conversation, until, halting and looking a little ashamed, she held up her drink to the bartender and pointed to Arthur. The man nodded, pulled a glass of foaming beer and handed to him. He held out a handful of coins to the widow who selected the right amount and paid the barman who was quite busy for a time serving other thirsty travellers. Arthur had the chance to look around. Although the majority of the customers were men, from the very young to aged grey-haired ones, there were a few women seated at the rough tables, some of them eating thick slices of bread with chunks of cheese from the plates set before them, chattering loudly between mouthfuls. The widow was again talking to the barman, who broke off the conversation with her, and turning to Arthur said in broken English:

"Welcome, sir. I am honoured to have an English gentleman drinking here in my humble bar. The next beer is on the house. I expect you are wondering why the widow Jaunta and I have so much to talk about. We were both born in the same village, so have been friends since childhood. She and her husband always used my bar when they came into the town shopping. This is the first time that she has been back since he died. We were all very sorry to hear the sad news and are pleased to see her looking so well. She tells me you are staying as a guest in her cottage. That is good. She is a very kindly woman, and deserves a little happiness."

He moved away to serve more customers, and when he returned he refilled the glasses of Arthur and the widow saying, "Please have a drink with me". A table had been vacated, so they moved to it and sat down. The beer was a cool and pleasant drink; he was about to move when a well-proportioned grey-haired woman came and sat in the empty seat, and opened a rapid conversation with the widow. Arthur rose and went over to the barman to enquire where the toilets were. "Through that door and yours is on the right."

Arthur was pleased to find it reasonably clean, and returning to the bar he thanked the barman who smilingly remarked:

"My name is Gregor, and that is my wife Lenie talking to the widow Jaunta. She has also known her for many years. When you have finished your shopping, please call in for a few moments and have another beer, before your bus leaves."

Arthur consulted his watch to find the time was nearing three o'clock. He pointed to his watch, saying, "We must hurry or I shall miss the bank."

They finished their drinks, then left to get the shopping done. The bank was just round the corner and on the point of closing. He managed to cash some travellers' cheques, then walked across the street to find the widow haggling with a stallholder over some meat; she bought some pieces, then moved on to a vegetable stall where onions and what appeared to be turnips were purchased. Then, taking his arm, she moved to the dairy produce stand. She spoke to the stallholder who cut off a small portion of each of the cheeses on display, and handed them to Arthur. After tasting the samples he pointed to three which he liked. The widow bought a piece of each, then ordered a good sized piece of a bright yellow cheese apparently her own choice. Strolling round and weaving in between the stalls they came upon one displaying rolls of soft materials. The widow stopped to admire the array of beautiful colours, seeming to like particularly one which she looked at longingly and stroked caressingly. Arthur could see she liked it and thought what a pretty frock it would make, being a warm cream shade, patterned in lovely blue flowers. He indicated the material to the stallholder, pointed to the widow, and held out some notes in their currency. He was quick to understand, and taking a tape measure from his pocket quickly took her measurements, then, unrolling the material, cut off the amount required to make her a dress. Before wrapping it he added a reel of matching cotton for the stitching, and a long length of blue ribbon for trimming. The look of amazement on her face caused Arthur to smile at her with satisfaction, and tuck the parcel under his arm. Taking the basket from the widow, which was now fairly heavy with the purchases they had made, he looked at his watch and pointed to the bus stop. It was nearing departure time for the bus back home.

On reaching the bus stop they saw that most of those waiting were the same people who had come to the town with them earlier. If he could find it, Arthur had one more purchase to make. Placing the basket down beside the widow he pointed across to the row of shops opposite, held up five fingers to indicate five minutes, and dashed over. Yes, the nearest shop was a grocery store. As he entered a young girl spoke to him. He shook his head, looked around, then spoke to the girl, saying, "Tea". She looked bewildered. "Tea," he repeated, pointing to the shelf containing coffee, and shaking his head, "I wish to buy tea". Her face brightened as she understood and she led him to another shelf, where there was an abundance of packets of tea. Picking up two packets he held out a handful of money; the girl took the amount needed to pay for the items. Glancing through the window, Arthur saw the bus waiting, and the widow signalling to him to hurry. He ran over, dodging in between the traffic on the road. Stepping up into the bus they found a front seat and sat down side by side.

Chapter Four

Arthur placed the basket on the floor between his feet, the parcel across his knees, and settled down to enjoy the return journey home. Then he remembered they had not gone back to the bar before leaving, to have a final beer. Never mind he thought, we are sure to be going into town again in a week or two, and can call in and apologise for failing to say goodbye. The return journey was as bumpy and tiring as the one to town had been, but they managed to relax a little; most of the passengers seemed to drop off to sleep. The bus stopped at a number of places along the route, passengers leaving in twos and threes, and it was nearing five thirty p.m. before they reached their destination. Helping the widow down, they started to walk towards the cottage. Hearing his name called, Arthur turned to see the priest hurrying after them, his cassock flying around him like the wings of a large blackbird. When he caught up with them, breathless from hurrying, he was unable to speak for a few moments, then haltingly enquired if they had enjoyed their outing.

"Oh! yes," Arthur remarked, "and I even managed to buy some tea. We English, as perhaps you know, drink more tea than coffee, so we shall now be able to enjoy an occasional change."

"Good, and were you able to change your money?"

"Yes," replied Arthur, "I trust I shall now have sufficient to last until our next visit to the town."

The widow now spoke to the priest, pointing to the parcel which Arthur still held under his arm. She spoke at some length and when she paused, the priest turned to him in surprise saying, "The widow Jaunta is rather puzzled as to why you have bought materials, cottons and ribbons, hardly the sort of thing for a man to wear." Arthur laughed and explained how, when he saw her looking so longingly at the pretty material, he guessed she would like to have a frock made from it:

"So I purchased enough material for her to sew one up, in time perhaps for our next visit to the town."

"How very generous you are," he exclaimed. "That is most kind of you," and turning to the widow explained what the contents of the parcel were for. She gazed open mouthed, first at the priest, then at Arthur. She blushed and smiled, then without any warning ran and put her arms around him, and planted a light kiss on his cheek. It was now Arthur's turn to blush. The priest smiled, saying, "Away with you both, it is time for your evening meal. I will see you tomorrow morning Arthur, and don't forget the papers and photograph; we can perhaps begin to unravel this mystery and provide some answers to your quest. Come along about nine thirty, and bring a little tea with you, and I will try and make you a drink; I have no such thing as a teapot, as is used by the British people. Never mind, there must be something we can find in which to brew your tea, one of my parishioners went to town today and brought me back some supplies from the market, so I now have some sugar. See you tomorrow," and with that he turned and went towards the church.

Arthur and the widow continued on their way to the cottage arriving to find the hens and rooster, still busily scratching around the front garden. Unlocking the door, she went straight through to the kitchen, coming out with the old bucket containing the poultry food. Placing the basket and parcel on the table, Arthur took the food from her. Going outside he scattered it to the poultry and filled the old tin bowl with fresh water. Going indoors he heard the widow in the kitchen preparing the evening meal. She suddenly burst into song, the tune was cheerful and her voice was soft and clear. He stood and listened for a while. He had no idea of the meaning of the words, but it sounded like one of their folk songs. He went to his room and could still hear her singing. This made him feel very pleased, as it would seem that he had made her happy, if only for a short time. After washing his face and hands, he put on a clean shirt, the other one being dusty and sticky from the journey. He came down to find the table laid for two. Each had a plate containing slices of cold meat, a hunk of cheese, and a large plate of freshly sliced bread, butter in a dish, sugar in a bowl, a jug of milk and two mugs. Picking up one of the packets of tea, the widow held it out to Arthur and pointed to the kitchen. Realising that she was asking him to show her how to make the tea, he went with her to the kitchen, where he brought a kettle of water to the boil, found a jug into which he put some of the tea leaves, and when the kettle reached the boil, he filled the jug with the boiling water. Placing a small plate on top, he carried it to the table. Sitting down they started to eat; moments later she pointed to the jug, and lifting the lid which covered it Arthur picked up his spoon and stirred the contents. He waited a few moments then carefully poured some tea into his mug. After adding milk and sugar he tasted it, then filled the mug. He then proceeded to fill the other mug, but the widow held his hand when he was about to put the sugar in. She shook her head and took a careful sip at the tea, watched Arthur do the same, smiled and nodded then drank some more. "So she likes tea," he thought.

Finishing the meal, they drank the last of the tea and Arthur helped to remove the dishes from the table. Putting the used tea leaves into the food for the hens, he went to the sink to do the washing up, but the widow held his arm and shook her head, so going into the garden he sat on an old chair where, resting in the rays of the setting sun, he dozed off to sleep, waking with a start to find it was getting dark and the widow had already lit the lamp inside. He rose, stretched, and going into the cottage, found the widow with the material he had bought her, spread out on the table, measuring it by laying an old frock on it, saying something to Arthur which he did not understand. She then sat down and with a small sharp knife, began to unpick the old frock. Arthur watched her nimble fingers at work. Soon the pieces were laid out on the material, leaving plenty of room to cut round. There was ample to make the new frock. She found a pair of scissors and began to cut out her new garment. When this was finished she indicated it was time for her to retire. Rolling up the material, she smiled and nodded saying goodnight in her own language. Then to his surprise added, "Good night Arthur," in English. He heard her in her room, and realised he too was feeling tired, so lighting a candle, he put out the lamp and also went upstairs. He noticed as he got into bed the clothing he had changed out of before dinner had been removed and guessed the widow had taken them to wash. He lay for some time thinking over the events of the day. They had enjoyed the outing and each other's company, despite the limitations of their conversations. The widow had been made happy with his small gift, so it could be considered to have been a very pleasant day.

His thoughts now turned to Gregor and his wife Lenie who seemed to be a devoted couple and he was pleased the widow had friends in the town. He remembered the beer they had been drinking, not too strong, refreshing, but a bit too sweet for his palate. He was looking forward to a few more glasses on their next visit to the town. The cool air touched him, as a breeze stirred the bedroom curtains. His mind now at rest, he gently relaxed and fell into a deep sleep.

When he awoke and checked the time, he found it was after eight a.m. The widow was already busy down below. He rose and went over to look out of the window. The weather did not look too kind this morning, dull with dark clouds, and a freshening wind, and he thought he heard the sound of thunder in the distance.

Quickly washing and shaving in the cold water from the jug he thought to himself, how lucky I brought with me a good supply of razors, cold water soon takes the edge off them. Dressing in the attire he had worn the previous evening, he went downstairs to find the breakfast table laid and, most surprising, a jug of tea brewing beside his plate. She watched a little anxiously as Arthur poured himself a mugful, at the same time saying "Good morning".

She replied "Good morning" in English, and after a moment's hesitation, asked, "Tea, good, yes?"

Arthur nodded, it was quite good. She had evidently watched carefully how he had done it the night before. Filling her mug and handing to her they sat down to eat breakfast in silence. When the meal was finished Arthur picked up his plate and mug and took them to the kitchen, then seeing the time realised he would have to leave now for his appointment with the priest. Going to his room, he looked out the papers and photograph. Placing them safely in his inside pocket he went to find the widow who was now busy in the back garden weeding the vegetable patch.

"I am going to see the priest," he told her, "and will be back by six o'clock." She nodded that she understood, then pointing upwards to the dark clouds went inside and returned with an umbrella which she handed to him. Thanking her with a smile, he set off for the church. This is it, he thought, I wonder if there will be a successful outcome from today's discussions.

When about halfway on his journey the first spots of rain began to fall and again the distant rumble of thunder could be heard. He put up the umbrella and noticed, with a grin, it was torn in several places. "However, it will keep some of the rain off me," he thought as he hurried on. The priest must have been watching his approach as the door opened immediately he reached it, and with a smile of welcome the priest remarked:

"It looks as if we are about to have another storm." Putting the umbrella in a corner he placed his hat on the handle; entering the sitting room his usual chair was offered to him and the priest sat facing him with a look of interest and anticipation on his face.

"I hope you remembered to bring the papers and photos with you." Reaching into his inside pocket, Arthur removed the large envelope and handed it to the priest who held it for a moment or two as if not too eager to disturb the contents, then slowly opening it he extracted first the photograph, which he studied intently, turning it over to read the inscription on the back. "Oh! Yes, you guessed rightly about who they are, this is indeed the picture of Ivor Kaldev's mother and sister taken on May 23rd 1935 outside their cottage. His Mother's name is Guira, the sister is Stephany, apparently a very pretty girl who, as you say looks to be sixteen or seventeen years of age at the time this was taken."

Carefully laying aside the photo, he picked up the first of the documents which gave personal details of Ivor in his own language.

"This", the priest continued, "places his mother as his next of kin and his birth date as June 10th 1908, which made Ivor as you surmised thirty-seven years old when he died. His birth place is given as the town of Palkhov and that is a very long way from here."

Putting the paper down, he picked up the next one. This was the service record of Ivor, during military conscription in his own army unit. Reading slowly, pursing his lips now and then and sighing a little, he turned the paper over and began reading the other side. He suddenly let out a sharp "Oh!" and spoke some words in his own language. This startled Arthur who had been deep in thought. Looking alarmed he sat upright in his chair, saying, "What is it Father, is there something wrong?" The priest hesitated a moment before replying, "I am not sure. Did you decide to come to our little village, thinking it to be the place from which Ivor came, and you would therefore perhaps learn something about his family? I presume that to be the reason for your quest."

Arthur moved to the edge of his chair and leaned toward the priest with an anxious look on his face.

"Yes, I translated as I thought, the name of this village, and despite the many problems with visas and passports, and other travel difficulties I decided to embark from this point, in an endeavour to trace any living relative of my late friend, and hopefully carry out his last wishes. Don't tell me I am on a wild goose chase, and wrong in my suppositions."

"I'm afraid so," he remarked, holding the document towards him. He pointed to a word halfway down the page. "You have misinterpreted the name of his home town. Ivor was born in Palkhov, but he and his family lived in a smaller town some twenty kilometres from there, and according to this paper had lived in the same cottage for generations. I can see how you came to make the mistake, as the names of the two places are very similar, but this is not the village you want, the name of which is Misakev not Mirmskov."

He went across to his desk returning with the map that had been used earlier to point places out to Arthur, and spreading it out on the table, they both spent some time studying the map in silence, peering closely at the worn and creased surface. Moving his fingers gently over it, the priest exclaimed, "Ah! here it is." Keeping his finger on a small spot close to the top of the map, he said, "Misakev, that was Ivor's home town. It is a very long way from here in an area difficult to reach, as there is very little transport between the two places. I also regret to say, it is a very troubled part of our country. War has been going on there for some time now, and it seems the Government are powerless to stop it. Two factions are fighting each other for control of the area, and as you can see from the map, it is mountainous and arid. Why they fight for such a barren place, I am at a loss to understand. Probably it is more of a tribal feud than the desire to conquer land."

"So, my friend, you can see the huge problem you are facing. Coffee?" he asked and leaving the map on the table went off to make it. Arthur made a careful study of the map during his absence. Yes, it was certainly a long way from here, with no sign of a railway going in that direction and the roads marked on the map were very sparse. Father Procovitch came in carrying the coffee pot and two mugs. He moved the map to one side, poured out the coffee, and when they each had a mug, he sat down again saying, "Let's have a look at the other papers."

He picked them up and read them intently. "Well," he remarked, "there is no doubt that Ivor was a good soldier. He has a very good record for when he did his national service here, and was also a good catholic. His parents were the owners of quite a large farm. It would appear that his father was killed in an accident soon after Ivor had completed his national service, so with the help of his mother and sister, he managed the farm. Having attended the school in Palkhov where he was born, he had been given a fairly good education, and was able to speak some Russian and English too, so, in that part of the world he was a well-educated man. That is why he was a member of the local council, and a leader of the farmers' cooperative."

Having read through the papers, he put them down and picked up Ivor's identity book. Flicking through the pages he noted a blank space, where the photograph should have been. Showing the blank space to Arthur he asked, "Did you remove this?"

"No, it was missing when he handed them to me."

"What a pity," he remarked. "A picture of him would have been a great help to you. Perhaps when you reached his home town, it might have triggered off someone's memory of him." Looking through it again, he was about to place it with the other things, but when he opened the inside of the back cover feeling the surface, he stopped, saying, "There is something here between the lining and the cover."

He went to his desk and picked up a paper knife. Inserting it beneath the lining he carefully peeled it back to disclose the identity photo of Ivor which had been successfully hidden and was still in good condition. "Is this his photo?" asked the priest. "Yes, that is Ivor," Arthur replied. "I wonder why he hid it between the covers, he must have had a very good reason for doing so."

They finished the coffee, and noticed that the rain had stopped and the sun was making a feeble attempt to emerge from behind the clouds. Sitting for a while deeply immersed in their own thoughts, the priest was the first to break the silence. "Well, what can we do now, it is a long journey to that part of our country; travelling will be most difficult, and I have no idea of the conditions there, or even, in view of the trouble in the region whether you can safely reach the town."

Arthur looked a little downcast but the priest got up, saying, "Let's have some lunch, then look at all possibilities. There must be a solution."

Going to the kitchen he returned bearing a tray with two plates of bread and cold meat, a pot of freshly made hot coffee, clean mugs and cutlery. After the frugal meal he remarked, "Now let us try to sort out some way of getting you to Misakev, otherwise it looks as if your quest ends right here."

The priest now asked Arthur how things were going at the cottage, and how the widow was getting on with her English. "Quite well," answered Arthur. "She can pronounce a number of words already, and I have learnt a few words of your language also, so we are making headway; at least we understand each other better now than when I first arrived. She is such a kind and happy-natured person. I am surprised that some local widower has not snapped her up, she is a good cook and housewife, and has a comely figure."

"You are not far wrong," the priest replied. "There have been one or two suitors trying to move in with her, but they have all been turned away. I think she still feels her loss too deeply, and she is a very independent person, but if the right man came along I am sure she would marry again, but that could be some time away."

"Is there a post office in the village?" Arthur asked.

"No, the nearest one is in the market town, to which you went yesterday. Did you wish to post a letter?"

"Yes. I must get news to my Nephew. I promised to let him know where I was, and what was happening so by now I expect he will be getting worried."

"Write a letter and let me have it. I know you are not a catholic, even so you can take part in our service so come along with the widow Jaunta to Mass tomorrow. A fellow priest will be taking me in his car to the town on Monday, where we have some matters on religion to discuss, also some new decrees from our bishop to be conducted. I will post your letter for you, and if you wish to, please use my address for any return mail whilst you are here."

"Thank you," replied Arthur, "I will accompany the widow to Mass tomorrow, then we must start looking into ways and means of getting me to the other part of your country. There is no time limit to my being over here, but I would like to get my quest finished before the onset of winter. I understand the winters here are quite severe, so I would rather be back in England before then."

The priest nodded saying, "Yes, that is true, and I am sure this is costing you a great deal of money, travelling these days is very expensive."

Once they were both again settled in their chairs he continued, "Firstly, you will need a contact. There is sure to be a priest in

Misakev, I will give you a letter of introduction to him. It may be possible for him to find you suitable accommodation, and if he has been there for a considerable length of time, he might even assist in tracing the family you seek, that is, if any of them are still alive. The hardest part will be finding a method of transport, to get you to the town."

Chapter Five

Going to his desk he rummaged around for a minute or two and came upon an old railway timetable.

"It is well out of date, but it will at least tell us if there is a rail link to that area." He studied it for some time, turning pages over and checking with the map. He looked up. "Well, my Son, all I can discover from this out of date timetable, assuming the trains still run to there, is that you can, by changing four times on the journey, get to this town here. He pointed to a place on the map. "This is just over halfway from this village to the place you wish to reach. From there, you will have to rely on road transport, there must be buses running between the towns. If you could make your way to the motor roads, you might perhaps get a lift in a lorry." He stopped speaking, and sat awaiting a reply.

Arthur, sorting matters out in his own mind, realised the overwhelming difficulties he still faced. It had taken quite a lot of planning to get even this far, but he knew he had to finish the job he had started for his own satisfaction and peace of mind.

"I think we shall have to plan this with the greatest care," he remarked. The priest agreed. "Leave it to me. I will make enquiries as to what the transport situation is. After reaching the end of the rail system, I can do that by contacting my fellow priests residing in some of the towns leading up to Misakev. Replies may take some time, as our postal system is not very good. I will check the records of names in the church register, and write to them within the next few days. Some of the names may have been changed with time, but that will not be too difficult. I am sure that all who can, will help."

Arthur glanced at his watch, saying, "Thank you Father. That is as far as we can get today. I will return to the cottage now. You must have plenty to do in preparation for your services tomorrow, I will bring my letter for you to post when we attend Mass."

With that he rose, and picking up his umbrella and hat, shook hands with the priest and left. The sun was now shining, and it was quite warm, he strolled along enjoying the fresh air of eventide. He arrived at the cottage to find the widow busy with needle and cotton making the material up into a new dress. She smiled at him, holding up the partly finished garment, which had all the appearance of becoming a very pretty dress. Arthur returned the smile, as he went up to his room, replacing the documents in his case. Refreshing himself with a good wash, he noticed his clean shirt and underwear neatly ironed and folded on the chair beside his bed. He packed them away, and went down to the living room. The widow was still sewing; he watched her fingers moving with dexterity, making small neat stitches. It reminded him of his childhood, when his mother would sit sewing in the evening; what she made all those years ago, he had no idea, but she had the same neat action in her sewing as the widow.

She looked at the clock, which pointed to five p.m. She held up six fingers saying in English, "We eat at six, yes?" Arthur agreed, and leaving her to her sewing, went outdoors to sit on the old log and watch the hens scratching around the garden.

His thoughts centred on the coming expedition he was about to embark upon and the ensuing problems which might arise as a result. Sleep must have taken him over, for the next thing he knew was being gently shaken by the widow and being told the meal was ready. She had made both tea and coffee; the food was simple but tasty, the tea most welcome. They sat and ate in silence. Suddenly remembering his promise to the priest to attend Mass the next day, Arthur knelt down, making a sign as if in prayer, then going to the clock he pointed to the letter ten, saying:

"Mass at ten." Looking puzzled for a moment, the widow then realised what he was trying to say. She smiled at him saying in perfect English:

"Yes, tomorrow we go to Mass." When the meal was finished and the table cleared, Arthur undertook the task of washing the dishes, to enable the widow to proceed with her sewing.

Arthur went to his room returning with a writing pad and envelopes, then sat down at the table to write to his nephew. There was a great deal to say, explaining to him that he was now in need of more money. Arrangements had been made at the bank for his nephew to undertake any business transactions during his absence abroad, and an agreement drawn up for him to obtain travellers' cheques and forward them if Arthur were in need, which was a much safer way than trying to have money transferred over here where the banking system appeared to be as outdated as so many of the other services. The widow glanced up at him now and then, watching with interest, as he sat quietly writing. For almost an hour, they were each engrossed in their own occupation, when Arthur realised the room was becoming gloomy. Reaching to the shelf for the lamp he placed it in the centre of the table, and lit it; she smiled at him and, bending closer over her material, continued sewing. Completing his letter, Arthur addressed the envelope, placing it aside to give to the priest the next morning. Plying her needle for a little while longer, the widow stood up and held the frock she was sewing close to her body, making a few adjustments here and there with pins. She then sat down again and continued with her work. As it was now quite dark outside, Arthur went to his room and brought down the book he was reading. They sat in silence, but were evidently enjoying each other's company.

Some time later, rising again, she shook out her new dress, looked at it from various angles then leaving it on the table, went into the kitchen from where Arthur could hear her raking ashes from the little cooking stove. A short while later she returned with a blanket over her arm and in her hand an old fashioned flat iron, held by a thick piece of old material. Laying the blanket flat on the table she proceeded to iron the dress carefully pressing the seams flat; when finished she held it up for his inspection. "Yes, it looks very nice, quite a pretty frock." He thought she understood his meaning, for she gave him a lovely smile, picked up the blanket and iron and took them to the kitchen.

Returning, she put away her sewing, looked at the clock and, seeing the time was well after ten p.m., turned to him saying, "Goodnight, my friend. I go to sleep."

Arthur was taken by surprise, she must have learned to say that in English, by listening to the priest and him talking.

"Goodnight," he replied, and the widow went up to her room; hearing her moving above, he decided it was time he also retired. Going upstairs he was about to enter his room, when he heard the widow call:

"Arthur?" She had left her bedroom door slightly open, and was saying something in her own language. He knocked on her door asking:

"Yes, what is it?" She came to the door, opening it wider, saying, "We eat at eight thirty in the morning." All she had on was a very coarse nightdress, her feet were bare, and her hair hung loosely around her. She stood looking at Arthur. Suddenly moving towards him, she threw her arms around his neck and pressed a firm kiss on his lips. He could feel the beating of her heart, and the pressure of her breasts hard against his chest. Releasing him she looked down at the floor, a deep flush suffusing her face.

Caught completely off guard, Arthur stood dumbfounded and a little confused, also blushing. Looking up at him again she turned back into her bedroom slowly closing the door behind her. He stood bewildered on the little landing, thinking, 'Good God, I do believe she is falling in love with me. This is a pretty kettle of fish. I had no idea this was going to happen. Perhaps the priest will explain to her that in a week or two, I shall be leaving to continue elsewhere, my quest to trace Ivor's family. This no doubt will be very upsetting for her.'

He got into bed but lay there unable to sleep, thinking of the widow, and the hurt it would cause when she learnt he was planning to leave. 'Maybe it is only friendship she feels for me, and thus enjoys my company; she is surely not expecting me to return her affections.' After tossing and turning for some time, he fell into an uneasy sleep, being disturbed by erotic dreams such as he had not experienced since his youth, as a result of which he awoke to find himself bathed in sweat. As it was still dark he lit his candle, sponged himself down with cold water, got back into bed, and with his mind now free from problems slept well. He awoke to find it was now 7.40 a.m. so, after a quick shave and wash, he dressed in his best suit, clean shirt and shoes, and went downstairs to breakfast.

As he entered the living room the widow came from the kitchen. Giving him a slight smile and saying "Good morning, Arthur," she placed before him the usual breakfast of bread and butter and the pot of tea. Coffee was her choice, and it was apparent the widow had already eaten so Arthur ate alone, whilst she went outside to feed the hens. When she came back she collected the used crockery and did the washing up. Returning, she pointed to the clock saying something to him which he took to mean that they must leave soon after nine o'clock for Mass.

The widow then went up to her room to change, leaving Arthur to sit and muse over the strange happenings of the previous night. It was a most embarrassing situation, he thought. 'I must admit to a certain warm feeling for her, she is a kind and comely woman with whom it would not be too difficult to fall in love, but I may not be able to come back here again, and I certainly could never live in this God-forsaken place; Ah! well, perhaps it is only a flight of fancy, maybe she was trying to show her appreciation for my gift to her.'

It was almost 9.15 a.m. when the widow entered the room. She was wearing her new dress trimmed with small blue ribbon bows all down the front. It fitted perfectly; she must have finished it in the early hours of this morning. Her shining hair was combed back and her face lightly powdered, with a touch of *rose sucre* lipstick, to emphasise a pretty mouth. Arthur sat and gazed at her in amazement.

The straw hat trimmed round the brim with blue flowers and a large blue bow with long ribbons hanging from the back, completed the outfit. In one hand she carried what Arthur thought was a prayer book. Stepping into the middle of the room, she slowly turned around, holding her arms away from her sides, then looked at Arthur questioningly, obviously asking for his approval. Arthur was lost for words by the change in her, with her sparkling eyes and the slight flush on her cheeks, she was transformed from an elderly widow to a smart middle-aged woman.

He stood up and took a deep breath, saying, "You look lovely," and from the look she gave him, he knew she understood his meaning. Going to the front door she stepped outside and held it open for Arthur to follow. Locking the door, she took hold of his arm and, in the cool of the morning, walked in silence towards the church, hearing the cracked bell on the church roof tolling more clearly, the nearer they approached. Other residents of the village were also winding their way to church, at the main door of which was the priest, welcoming his flock, as they entered. He looked with surprise at the widow; she blushed and smiled when he spoke to her. Turning to Arthur he said,

"I have never seen the widow Jaunta looking so lovely since she was a young woman. The frock she has made is very pretty; she must have worked very hard to finish it in time for Mass today, and what is the sparkle I see in her eyes? I do believe she is falling in love with you, my Son."

Arthur's face registered dismay, and he shook his head. "I hope not Father, I must leave here soon, and if that has happened it could break her heart."

"Never fear," replied the priest. "Perhaps it is only puppy love. Please find a seat. I must complete robing in readiness for the service." He hurried away. Seats were found for them about halfway down the centre aisle. As they sat down some of the congregation turned to look at them, nodding to the widow, who returned their nods.

The priest came to stand before the altar. They all stood whilst he spoke some words, which Arthur did not understand, then they all knelt during the saying of prayers, after which a hymn was sung, to the accompaniment of a squeaky harmonium, played by an elderly lady. This was followed by what seemed to be a Litany or Psalm, the bread and wine were blessed, and the congregation filed singly before the altar, to take holy communion. Taking Arthur's hand the widow led him forward and they took Communion together. Much to Arthur's surprise, the last hymn was announced in English.

"I have selected this in honour of our English friend, who is here with us today." This was repeated in his own language, and all eyes were now turned on Arthur. "Let us now sing *Fight the Good Fight.*"

Arthur sang lustily, and enjoyed the tune. Thus ended the service. After shaking hands with the priest, they left the church, and set off to walk back to the cottage.

Chapter Six

When they arrived home, the widow changed into her everyday clothes, carefully putting away the new dress, then went to the kitchen to prepare a light meal. Arthur noticed there was still a sparkle in her eyes and a smile on her face. It was evident she had enjoyed the morning outing. They sat in silence, and were about to drink their coffee, when the sound of a car was heard approaching and to the surprise of them both it stopped at the gate of the cottage. Arthur got up to look through the window to see who it could be. Peering over his shoulder the widow let out a squeal of pleasure as she recognised the driver. It was Gregor, the bar owner from the market town, and emerging from the passenger seat was his wife. The widow ran to the gate to welcome them and, as Arthur joined them, Gregor was handing a cardboard box from the boot of the car to the widow. He then lifted up another box and handed it to Arthur.

"Ah! most welcome," said he, seeing that the box contained a dozen bottles of beer. Lenie and the widow were deep in conversation. Gregor turned to Arthur saying, "We close the bar at one p.m. on Sundays, and as we did not see you again before you left for home on Friday, we decided to pay a visit this afternoon." When settled in comfort, Arthur sat and listened to the chatter of the other three, who evidently had plenty to discuss.

Gregor turned to Arthur saying, "Sorry, how are things going with our friend and yourself?"

"Very well," he replied, "although I have very little knowledge of your language, I have learnt a few words and we manage quite well, but there is now another problem facing me. As you will recall when I first met you, my reason for being here was to try and fulfil the dying wishes of one of your countrymen, who fought beside me in the last war. We became very good friends but he was fatally injured at the crossing of the Rhine. His last request was that I come here and try to find any of his family that might still survive, and tell them of his bravery."

"This I understand," said Gregor. "But what is the problem?"

"Well, according to Father Procovitch I have mistaken the name of the village where my friend Ivor Kaldev lived. I thought it was this village of Mirmskov, but when the priest translated his documents, it seems that the village I want is Misakev, and that it is way up in the north of your country, and from all accounts is a trouble spot, with a civil war going on there. It would also seem to be a difficult part to reach, as there is a noticeable lack of rail and road transport."

Gregor studied the map. "Oh! dear," he remarked, "you are quite right. It is, as you say, a long way from here, and very difficult to get to and with the added danger also of the warring factions, you will have much trouble getting to his home village. However the priest and I between us may be able to help. Please come and visit us on the next market day, and I will give it much thought. Catch the first bus into the town and we will expect you just before midday for lunch. On market days the bar opens from ten thirty .a.m. to two thirty p.m. then from four p.m. until ten p.m., so there will be time for us to see if we can iron out some of your problems."

Taking a deep breath, Arthur said, "One thing you can do for me while you are here: I have to somehow inform the widow of my intention to leave here, and try to get to the right place. Would you explain this to her? If she understands my predicament, she will perhaps realise that as soon as my plans are completed, I shall be leaving."

"Yes, I will do that," he remarked, and turning to the widow and his wife, began speaking to them both. Surreptitiously watching the widow, Arthur saw the look of disappointment that crossed her face as she gave him a worried look but when Gregor had finished, she smiled and spoke to him. Gregor translated for her. "widow Jaunta understands your quest is important to you. She is saying that she wishes you good luck and a safe journey, and asks that when you have completed your mission, would you come back to see her, even if it is on your way back to England just to say goodbye."

"Of course I will," replied Arthur. "Please explain to her that I hope to stop here on my return journey, for at least a day or two. That is the least I can do, to thank her, the priest and you and your wife for your kindly help and hospitality, and while I think of it, please give me your address and telephone number, so that I can keep in touch. If there is a postal service in the area I will write to you all, and keep you up to date with my progress."

The ladies were chatting away, no doubt about Arthur's intended journey and other matters with which they were concerned. Gregor went into the kitchen, returning a short while later with some bottles of beer and a plate containing sandwiches which they had prepared and brought with them. the ladies broke off their conversation and joined the two men at the table. The beer was cool, the food tasty, and after enjoying the light meal, the ladies continued to chatter. Gregor turned his attention to Arthur telling him that, although money was short in the area, the bar was giving them a fairly good living.

"Our community are mostly farm labourers, none of them earning very big wages but being thrifty, when the opportunity arises for them to visit the market town, they have sufficient money to spend on enjoying a few glasses of beer, which is of course to our advantage.

"I bought the car a few weeks ago from a friend no longer able to afford the upkeep of it. It was in poor condition when I bought it but another friend, a mechanic, has managed to make it roadworthy. We find it most useful for picking up extra beer from the brewery when stocks are running low, handy for visiting our family more often, and we shall be able to come and see the widow occasionally."

Arthur nodded. "I too have a car back in England. It is almost impossible these days to get about without one. Although we have plenty of transport running to various parts of the country, a car is much more useful as you can get to your destination without the hassle of waiting for trains and buses, which never seem to be on time these days."

When the last of the sandwiches were eaten, and the beer bottles empty, Gregor stood up saying, "We must go now, as the bar has to be opened this evening. We have enjoyed our visit and hope to come again."

They all went outside. Lenie kissed the widow on the cheek, held out her hand to Arthur then, changing her mind, reached up and kissed his cheek. Gregor laughed, and called Arthur over to the car, where he handed him a box containing a dozen bottles of beer. "For you, and the widow of course." Leaning forward he whispered, "I don't suppose you have realised that the widow is falling in love with you. When the ladies were talking she did not say as much, but I can see it in her eyes whenever she looks at you. I do not expect you ever thought of this happening did you?"

"Oh dear no!" said Arthur, "neither did I set out to let it happen. It is a most difficult situation, but I must defuse it in the best way possible."

Gregor then spoke to his wife. She gave the widow a final hug, then shook hands with Arthur, saying, "Come and see us next market day." Getting into the car, and calling their goodbyes to each other, they drove away.

Standing by the gate, they watched until the car was out of sight, then went back into the cottage, the widow going straight into the kitchen to wash up the crockery that had been used. Arthur picked up his book and sat down to do a little reading, listening to her moving about in the kitchen. He then thought he heard her crying. He crept quietly to the door to see the widow, trying with little success to keep at bay the tears streaming down her face, with the corner of her apron. Moving away silently without her seeing him he sat down again, feeling very unhappy. He had no idea that she had nurtured a secret affection for him. He sat there pondering on this latest turn of events, failing to see how the problem was to be overcome. When the widow came back into the room she had ceased crying but her eyes were red rimmed, and her smile a little wan. She sat and faced Arthur speaking rapidly to him; he surmised she was trying to explain why she was so upset. About to take her hands in his to comfort her, he realised that such a gesture might be misconstrued, so refrained from touching her, but smiled to reassure her that he did not wish to cause her any distress. "Surely she understands this," he thought.

Soon afterwards she went out to feed the chickens. He then heard her in the vegetable garden at the back, so went out to offer his help. She was digging up potatoes. Taking the fork from her he lifted some roots. She accepted his help, picked up the potatoes, cleaned off the loose earth and, placing them in her basket, went indoors. Arthur followed. She was in the kitchen preparing the evening meal so, picking up his book, he sat down and continued to read. After the meal they spent the time in convivial silence, he reading, she doing her sewing. He was not sure whether Gregor and Lenie had fully explained to the widow that he would be leaving in a short time, travelling on, in an endeavour to fulfil the dying wishes of his late friend, so he decided to see Father Procovitch tomorrow and ask him if he would try and soften the blow for her, when the time came for him to depart. He looked at the widow, who was now putting away her sewing and yawning. She glanced at the clock indicating to Arthur she was ready to retire. Smiling, he nodded his head. She left and he soon heard her moving about in the room over head. After spending a few more moments reading, he decided he also would retire, and go and pay a visit to the priest in the morning in order to discuss his present problem. Lighting his candle, he put out the lamp, and went quietly to his bedroom.

He noticed when passing the widow's room that the door had been left half open and she was standing in the candle light wearing only her nightgown, and brushing her lovely hair. Arthur hesitated, she came and stood before him, the shy smile and clear look of invitation in her eyes was most suggestive, as though she wished him to share her bed. The prospect was an exciting one; she was an attractive woman and it had been some time since he lost his wife and had slept alone with no one to cuddle up to.

Feeling his body heat rising, he realised he must restrain himself. He turned and entered his own room. Removing his clothes, he got into bed, his thoughts tumbling about like leaves in the wind making it difficult to sleep. When sleep finally overtook him, he was plunged into the depths of his subconscious mind, bringing dreams such as he would have preferred not to have experienced. Into these came his late wife clad in her silky nightdress. Bursting with loving desire, she stood beside the bed gazing down on him and leaning over began to stroke his hair. Having always enjoyed the closeness of each other's bodies, their sex life had been perfect harmony; climbing into bed she snuggled up to him. He was aroused and woke with a start. Sitting up in bed, he found he had an erection. "Good God," he exclaimed aloud. "I must be returning to my youth again. This will never do; the sooner I leave here the better it will be for my conscience." He allowed himself a wry smile, and after cooling down he dropped off into a dreamless sleep.

Looking at his watch on awaking, he found it was only seven a.m. His mouth felt very dry, so slipping on his dressing gown, and noticing the widow's door was now firmly closed, he assumed she was still sleeping. He crept quietly downstairs to get a glass of water.

It was a clear sunny morning with little wind; the air being fresh and clean, taking a deep breath, he went into the room, and as he entered he heard a gasp of surprise, and to his amazement and discomfort saw the widow standing naked in a large tin bath, obviously having a strip wash. Looking shocked she made to grab the bath towel laying on the nearby table. She reached it but not before Arthur had taken a view of her body; her breasts, though on the large size, were firm for a woman of her age. She had well rounded hips, a flat belly, and unblemished skin. Arthur turned away, blushing for the first time in many years. The widow by now had managed to cover her nudity, and she also was blushing. He backed out of the room saying, "Sorry, I had no idea you were up. Please forgive me," and as he closed the door to return to his bedroom, he was certain there was a faint chuckle of laughter from her. He did not feel like going back to bed, so sat thinking things over until he heard her come up to her room and close the door. He quickly washed shaved and dressed, and went down to find his breakfast laid out for him. Coming in later, she smiled and blushed a little, then sat down.

Arthur explained, by a few words and hand signals that he was going to the church, to speak to the priest. she seemed to understand and, taking the dirty dishes, went into the kitchen. Saying, "Cheerio," he set off to walk to the village, but when he arrived at the church the priest could not be found, and there was no answer to his knock on the door of the private quarters. Turning and going round to the church, he entered but there was no one inside. He might be back later he thought, I will take a walk and wait a while. Strolling down the village street he met a few customers leaving the bakery with newly baked loaves of bread, and decided to take one home with him. Whilst being served he noticed a dish of buns, or cakes on the counter. Pointing to them, he held up four fingers to the shopkeeper who nodded and placed four buns in a paper bag and, handing them over, spoke in his own language. Realising he was asking for payment, Arthur held out a handful of coins. The man smiled and took the required amount saying something which Arthur took to be thank you. Leaving the shop, he made his way to the end of the street, where he sat on a rough bench to watch some children playing football on the village green; his thoughts were, 'Kids are all the same the world over; given a bit of space and a football, they will provide their own fun.' The ball came rolling towards him. He got up and kicked it back. A curly-haired boy, about ten years of age, collected the ball on his foot, dribbled past two or three players, steadied himself, and kicked it straight between the two tins which made up the goal posts. The others all cheered, and play restarted. He took particular notice of the boy who had just scored the goal; he was very agile and had complete control of the ball. 'It looks like he will be an accomplished footballer when he is older,' he thought.

Arthur enjoyed watching the children for a while longer then, glancing at his watch saw it was nearly noon. He rose and went back to the church. The priest had not yet returned, so he sat in one of the pews feeling relaxed in the cool air. Within a short time he heard someone enter. Turning round he saw the priest approaching. "Hello!" he said. "How nice to see you. Is everything all right with you and the widow?"

"Yes," replied Arthur, "but I need a little advice on a personal problem concerning the widow and myself!"

Looking serious, the priest exclaimed, "I hope you have had no upsets with the widow Jaunta, she is a good woman."

"No," replied Arthur, a little too quickly thought the priest who, looking slightly puzzled, pointed to his private rooms, saying, "Let us discuss it in here, and see if I can be of help."

Entering the room Arthur sat in his usual chair, waiting for the priest to be seated then, taking a deep breath he began to explain his predicament with the widow, and the romantic notions that seemed to be entering into their relationship.

The priest listened, his face showing concern, and when Arthur had finished, said, "Don't worry, I will explain to the widow Jaunta that you have no designs on her, and the thought of a sexual relationship has never entered your head. I feel sure she will understand and also realise that when you eventually return to England, you will pick up your normal life again, and this adventure, which had to be undertaken, will I hope, be only a happy memory."

Satisfied with his reply, after drinking a cup of coffee with him, Arthur returned to the cottage, where the widow was once more busy in the garden. He went to his room to sort out his clothes, placing them ready for packing again as soon as the information he required was received from Gregor's friend and the priest.

After the evening meal they once again sat in silence, the widow busy with her sewing, Arthur engrossed in his book. The next morning with breakfast over, and the washing up out of the way, they worked together in the vegetable garden, he digging up potatoes, she cutting greens for dinner, and during this time someone was heard calling from the front of the cottage. Arthur went to see who it could be and there, astride his bicycle, was a youth with a letter in his hand, which Arthur saw was addressed to himself. He handed the boy some coins, who smiled and said thank you in his own language, and rode off back towards the village.

Chapter Seven

Seeing it was from England, he knew it would be an answer to the one he had sent to his nephew, so he went inside to read it and was assured that all was well at home. He was pleased to find enclosed a form from his bank to the local bank in the market town, giving them the authority to issue him with more travellers' cheques. He put the letter in his pocket to take into town the next day, when he could replenish his money and start to prepare for the journey further north.

Later that afternoon the priest arrived and had a long conversation with the widow. She looked a little distressed but after a while composed herself; the priest then spoke to Arthur. "I am sure the widow Jaunta now understands, there cannot be a romantic liaison between you. She is a little upset and disappointed, but realises that you will eventually be returning to England, when it would then have to end."

Thanking the priest for his kindness, Arthur smiled at her and thought, 'What a shame, under other circumstances, I might have been very happy to make her my companion.'

When the priest left they sat down to eat their evening meal in silence; they spent a quiet evening, each probably ruminating on the possibility of 'what might have been'; they decided to retire early in order to be up in good time to catch the first bus leaving for the market town. Arthur rose just after seven a.m., and found, on going downstairs, the widow was already preparing breakfast.

Dressed in her new frock, she looked cool and very smart. As soon as the meal was finished she cleared the table, and gathering up her basket and handbag, motioned to him that they would have to leave now if they were to catch the early bus. Walking briskly to the village they arrived just as the bus came into view, and boarding it, the only seating was at the rear, where they sat to enjoy the journey into the town. When alighting in the square the widow indicated she had some purchases to make at the market. Arthur went and presented his papers to the manager of the bank who, understanding a little English, soon completed the business, assuring him of help at any time, if it were needed. Shaking his hand Arthur thanked him and went to the counter to exchange some of the travellers' cheques for cash. He then went to look for the widow; this proved to be a simple matter as her pretty dress stood out like a shining star amidst the sombre attire of the many peasants. Seeing the amount of packages in her basket, he realised it must be heavy, so went over and took it from her to carry home. Going to the material stall, she bought some reels of cotton and other small items required for her sewing activities. As it was now nearing time for their visit to Gregor, they strolled through the crowd of shoppers up the lane, and into the bar. Seeing them enter Gregor waved them through to the rooms at the rear, where Lenie was preparing a cold meal for them. Leaving the two ladies talking, Arthur went back and seated himself at the bar, and accepting the beer Gregor handed him he tried in vain to hold a conversation with Gregor who was too busy serving customers with a thirst to quench. When the pace eased a little, he leant over the bar saying, "You will be pleased to know I have some useful information regarding your proposed trip to the north of our country. I will give you full details after I close for the afternoon."

The customers began to dwindle, leaving in ones and twos and at closing time only a few remained. After Gregor spoke to them, they also left. He then bolted the outer door. Arthur lent a hand collecting and washing the glasses, Lenie and the widow came to assist by emptying ashtrays and wiping the tables down, and when the place was clean and ready for opening in the evening, they sat down to enjoy the meal. Gregor brought in a bottle of his favourite wine which he stocked saying it was local produce. He poured out a generous amount for the widow and Arthur who both found it a pleasant and enjoyable wine. When the meal ended, the women gathered up the dishes, and disappeared into the kitchen with them, leaving the men to settle down in the two easy chairs, where Gregor began to tell Arthur of the progress being made in helping him to get to the village of Misakev.

"One of my friends has a son who is a long distance lorry driver and the company for whom he works sends deliveries of their goods to many places in the north of our country. Whilst not going to Misakev itself, he can possibly drop you within a hundred kilometres of it. He is prepared to take you along as a passenger to as far as is possible, and he would also like you to know that his vehicle is sometimes stopped and searched by the military, in case he might be trying to smuggle arms to either of the forces at war. You can rest assured that his company does not carry anything that might cause problems; he travels in that direction about once a month, and is scheduled to go into that region next Monday, leaving here very early. He will pick you up at five thirty a.m. Perhaps on the journey you can arrange something between you whereby he can pick you up again for the return journey on his next trip north in about a month's time, at (or near) the spot where he drops you off. He cannot be of further help as he has little knowledge of the area. From there, you will be on your own."

"That's great. I am almost ready to leave. Just a few more things to pack, and farewells to be said. The widow seems to have overcome her desire for me, and understands that I shall shortly be leaving."

They entered into further details about the impending journey, and soon realised it was time for Arthur and the widow to leave for their return home. When they arrived back at the cottage, the widow put away her purchases, laid the table, and prepared the evening meal which they once again ate in silence. She had been told by Gregor of the plans being made for his travels, and she looked quite sad. Arthur finished reading his book, making a mental note to give it to the priest, feeling sure that not only would he enjoy reading it, but it might help him with his English. Being tired after the lengthy outing of the day, they both retired early.

After breakfast the next morning, he managed to make the widow understand that he was visiting the priest and taking the book to him as a gift; she smiled and nodded her assent. The morning air was dry and cool. Arthur set off at a brisk pace reaching the church in record time to find the priest cleaning the silver fitments adorning the altar. "Good," he said, "I am so glad you are here. I was about to visit the cottage to see you. I have some useful information, of help to you in your quest."

Arthur replied, "I have also received some help from the bar owner in the market town," and he proceeded to inform the priest of the arrangements already made.

"How well that fits in with what I have had sent for you," replied the priest. "Come into my room and I will give you what I have." When they were seated, the priest took some papers from a large buff envelope, and studied for a few moments, then explained to Arthur, "These are letters from some of my brother priests living in areas you may have to visit. They all offer help and hospitality. The only village where a priest does not seem to reside is Misakev but that is not surprising as it has been the scene of some rather fierce fighting recently and no one seems certain of what present conditions are like there. However, here is a list of names and addresses of those willing to help along the way. Your driver friend will no doubt be passing through some of these towns and villages. Here also is my address and telephone number. Do not hesitate to contact me if you should be in trouble, I will do all in my power to help."

Producing a very old map, the priest pointed out the towns and villages with which he had contact, Arthur was surprised to see that some of them were not too far from the village he had to reach; they sat and talked about everyday matters and, as he left for the cottage, the priest wished him a safe and rewarding journey.

The next day being Sunday, attired in their best clothes they joined the villagers going to the church for Mass, during which the priest offered up a special prayer in English for Arthur's safety on his forthcoming journey. He felt a little humble at the concern of the priest and the widow, and made a vow to return, even if only for a few days, to thank them all, and let them know of his success or failure.

After the service many of the congregation spoke at length to the widow, then shook hands with Arthur. They wended their way slowly back to the cottage, and had a light meal. Changing into her old clothes, the widow attended to the needs of the chickens, then went to prepare the evening meal. Arthur divested himself of his Sunday best, and went to sit at ease in the garden, musing over the past events of the journey, and wondering what the future might hold in store. The evening meal was eaten in silence, then Arthur tried to explain to the widow that he would be leaving in the early hours of the following morning. After some thought, she nodded letting him know that she understood. In view of the early start next day, they both retired early, and he noticed as he went to his room that the door of her room was tightly closed. 'She has got the message,' he thought. 'I do hope I have not caused her too much heartache.'

It seemed only minutes after he put his head on the pillow that the widow was banging on his door calling his name, and he quickly rose, shaved, washed and dressed in his travelling attire and went downstairs, where he found his breakfast already on the table. It was now four thirty. Having eaten his breakfast, he went up to collect his few possessions, and when he returned the widow was waiting with a package which she handed to him, saying in broken English, "Food for your journey, and may God protect you."

She then spoke in her own language, and although Arthur could not translate it all, he knew she was asking him to come back and see her once more, before he left for England. Arthur nodded, picked up his cases and walked to the door, turning to say goodbye; the widow looked so unhappy, he hesitated, then putting down his cases he went to her, and putting his arms around her gave her a hug and kiss, to which she eagerly responded, then removed herself from his embrace. Arthur moved towards the gate leaving the widow standing there with tears streaming down her cheeks, which she made no attempt to hide. As Arthur reached the lane, she waved her hand and went back into the cottage.

Arriving at the spot where he was being picked up, Arthur was surprised to see the priest there also. He handed Arthur another envelope saying, "This came after you left on Saturday, it is another address to which you can turn for help if needed. I have come to thank you for coming to Mass yesterday, and wish you a safe journey. God go with you my friend, and take care."

They heard the sound of a heavy vehicle approaching; it drew up beside them and a virile young man jumped down from the cab. "My name is Joseph," he said, "and you must be Arthur, my father's friend Gregor has asked me to take you to the north. I only speak a little English, but I am sure we can make ourselves understood. We shall have to stop overnight at some places, but it will be with friends who will welcome you. Take the passenger seat, and let's be on our way, there is a long journey ahead before we can stop for the night."

Arthur took his seat, Joseph took the wheel and moving out of the village, they waved farewell to the priest, not knowing what to expect as they set out on the next part of Arthur's quest. The truck left the village in a cloud of dust. After traversing several miles of almost desolate terrain, Arthur began to have doubts in his mind as to whether he was doing the right thing. It was, to say the least, an

unknown quantity with the guerrilla warfare going on, the apparent
pitfalls in view, and the many unexpected encounters he was likely to
meet, but the dice had been thrown, and here he was, on his way to
fulfil a promise, made in the heat and noise of battle all those years
ago.

Discarding these thoughts, he sat back and looked at the driver,
with whom it was impossible to hold a conversation. For one thing,
Joseph's knowledge of English was limited and the engine was very
noisy; he had no idea what make of truck it was, but he thought
possibly of Russian manufacture. Although an old motor, it seemed to
be in fairly good condition. He also wondered what the trailer at the
back of the unit contained. He tried shouting above the noise of the
engine to ask Joseph what the load was that he carried.

He either did not hear or understand the question, as he proffered
no answer, so Arthur sat back and looked at the scenery. The area
was flat and uninteresting; the fields were parched and dry, and
despite the recent storms the crops looked stunted. There were few
trees or bushes to be seen, and here and there a farmhouse was set far
back from the road; it could not by any means of the imagination be
called a pretty part of the country.

After travelling for another half hour or so Joseph turned off the
narrow byway onto a wide made-up road with a fairly good surface,
on which there was quite a lot of traffic, trucks, cars, some coaches,
and now and then a farm cart with a horse labouring in the shafts,
trudging along ignoring the passing vehicles. Joseph kept up a steady
speed, and Arthur dropped off to sleep. He was suddenly awakened
by the truck pulling up to a standstill, and rubbing his eyes he looked
through the cab window and saw they had entered a small town.
Glancing at his watch he saw it was after ten thirty a.m. Good
Heavens! He had been asleep almost two hours. Joseph negotiated a
sharp turn and entered a large yard, one side of which was piled high
with wooden pallets, and making a U-turn he backed up to a long
loading bay. Three men came out of the building and directed him
where to back to and stop. He jumped off and Arthur heard the tail
board being lowered; returning to his cab he gently reversed the truck
up to the bay.

Switching off the engine he motioned to Arthur that he could get
out and stretch his legs for a while. Feeling stiff from the rigorous
journey, he took a walk to the rear of the trailer where the three men

were unloading crates. All bore the same markings which were not English. He jumped up onto the tail board to give a hand. Seeing his intention, Joseph called something to him, which he did not understand. He then called in English, "No, you must not help," so Arthur dropped to the ground, leaving the three men in dirty blue overalls to do the work. When thirty-six crates had been unloaded, another man wearing a white shirt and smart grey trousers stepped from a doorway on the bay with a bill board in his hand; checking the markings he counted the crates and handed the bill board to Joseph who, after signing and returning several papers, had one given back to him which he folded and put in his pocket. The three men waited for Joseph who turned to Arthur saying, "Come along, we can get refreshments here, but first I must close and lock the trailer." After securing the truck, he moved it from the bay; coming back the men were introduced, and shook hands all round. The teller led the way through a small door, which led into a large warehouse, with crates and boxes piled high in long rows. Walking through, some words in English caught his eye, and stopping to read them, he saw the inscription 'Glaxo dried milk'.

The next row was stencilled in large letters 'Prince's Tinned Ham, Prince's Foods, Liverpool', which revived past memories for Arthur. It became quite obvious to him that this was a food warehouse, and following Joseph and the three men, they at last came to a door, which apparently led into the canteen. Seating themselves at a long table, a cup of coffee was handed to each of them by a young girl of about sixteen or seventeen years of age; she then spoke to them and took the orders. Soon plates of meat in gravy which looked like a goulash, were put before each man; dishes of mashed potatoes, and swedes or turnips plus a plate of thick slices of bread were then placed on the table; the men helped themselves then started to eat, rather noisily, picking up their knives and forks. Arthur joined in, not realising, until the food appeared, how hungry he was. When the meal was finished and the table cleared, the three men lit up their strong smelling cigarettes. As Arthur and Joseph were non-smokers, they decided to leave. As they did so, the man who had checked the consignment came in and spoke to Joseph who then introduced Arthur to him. "I speak a little English," exclaimed the man, "I am the manager of the warehouse. We are import and export merchants. I hope you enjoyed our hospitality, to which you are most welcome.

Delivery drivers are always given a meal if they are here around lunchtime."

"Thank you," said Arthur, "it was most kind of you." (Thinking, 'we can eat the sandwiches the widow prepared later in the day.') They called goodbye to the men, went through the warehouse, and boarded the cab in preparation for continuing the journey. Before Joseph started the vehicle, Arthur asked him why he had not been allowed to help the men unload the goods. Joseph smiled at him, then in broken English explained that they had a very strong union, and no one outside it was allowed to do the work, and that was the only way they could protect their jobs, which were few and far between. If he had helped, it might have caused problems. Arthur understood, and made a mental note not to offer his services again.

They left the town, joining the same road by which they had entered it and drove steadily along. It was now well past noon. Joseph had yet another delivery to make before the end of the day, so he speeded up a little in order to reach his destination before they closed. Traffic was much lighter now and he was able to gain time. They passed through many small villages and had no occasion to stop, except for the call of nature. The countryside was much more pleasant; wooded areas were beginning to appear on the horizon. They were soon driving through a vast forest. This, thought Arthur, was much more interesting scenery than the flat plains they had passed through this morning. Entering a large town just after four p.m. Joseph went to another warehouse to unload more of his goods.

The routine was the same as before, with the men waiting to unload, the checker making sure that the delivery was correct, and Arthur making sure this time that he made no attempt to help. He just strolled around the yard to stretch his legs until the unloading was completed. When this was finished, Joseph signed the paper, and signalled to Arthur that they were now ready to leave. Climbing back into the cab they drove through to the other side of the town, where Joseph pulled into a small street, explaining to Arthur that an overnight stay would be made here. Picking up their bags, Joseph locked and checked his vehicle, then led Arthur to a house at the bottom of a short alley. "This is the home of one of my friends," he told Arthur. "He is also a driver and stays with us when he comes to my part of the country. His wife is a good cook. I am sure they will be pleased to meet you, and happy to offer you a meal and a bed for the night."

As they approached the door it was flung open, and a slim attractive young woman stood there with a big smile of welcome on her pretty face. She kissed Joseph on both cheeks, then realising he was not alone, blushed, and began talking excitedly to him. Joseph replied, and turning to Arthur remarked, "This is Gerda my friend's wife. I have explained to her who you are, and she welcomes you into her home. Karl, her husband will be home later."

Chapter Eight

They entered the house, and Arthur was surprised to see how comfortably it was furnished, even to a television set in one corner. Gerda left them for a few minutes, and returned with two bottles of beer, which she opened, pouring the contents into two glasses. She offered one to each man. The beer was cold and strong, a most welcome drink after their long dusty drive. Joseph and Gerda were deep in conversation – about what, he had no idea, but before long she looked at him, then back to Joseph, who managed to convey her meaning to Arthur. "She will show you to your room, and if you wish you may have a bath; a meal will be served when Karl gets home, and later this evening we are taking you out to see the town and have a few beers at our favourite bar."

"Good," said Arthur, and picking up his bag, followed Gerda upstairs where he was shown. overlooking the back garden, a small room, next to which was a bathroom. He unpacked his bag and after shaving, ran a bath and soaked for some time. He could hear the friends talking together. Whilst drying himself, he heard another voice enter the conversation. 'That must be the husband Karl,' he thought.

Having completed his ablutions, and attired in clean clothes he went down to the sitting room. Yes, Karl had arrived home; his wife was busy in the kitchen preparing the evening meal. Karl was introduced to him and spoke a few words in his own language, having no knowledge of English. Joseph with his slight use of English, was able to translate, "Karl also makes you welcome in his home."

He handed round more beer; they all sat down and the two men chattered away in their own language for some time. Arthur sipped his beer; his bones ached from the long bumpy journey and he was glad to be able to relax. Although not understanding the conversation, he surmised that Joseph was telling his friend the purpose of his journey to this part of their country. Glancing in his direction occasionally, they continued their animated talk, until Gerda, having laid the table for a meal, came in with the food. Seating themselves round the table, Gerda served them with meat and vegetables. Arthur's first taste of the meat proved it to be very tender steak. The three spoke to each other during the meal, and when Joseph asked Arthur if he was enjoying it, he nodded and smiled at Gerda, who returned his smile.

The first course finished, Gerda cleared the table, and brought back from the kitchen a large fruit pie and a jug containing a liquid, serving a good piece of pie to each one, the pastry of which was very good and the fruit delicious. The sauce poured over it was sharp, sweet and spicy, and noticing Arthur's interest in the sweet Joseph tried to explain to him that it was a speciality of the region. Arthur thanked them for a meal he had certainly enjoyed, and which was followed by a cup of good coffee, after which the two men disappeared upstairs to prepare for the evening's outing, whilst Arthur relaxed once more in the comfortable easy chair.

Gerda came in from the kitchen and switched on the television. It was the News Report, and Arthur had difficulty in understanding the words, but had a good idea of what was happening from the pictures being shown. Soldiers in battle dress were being depicted fighting amid a back drop of mountain scenery. It was obvious this was the guerrilla war that was being fought further north of the town, where they now were, and just before the programme ended, Joseph came in and turned to Arthur, saying, "It is going to be very difficult for you. They are the fighters, and that is the war zone through which you have to pass, to get to your destination." Arthur felt a cold shiver run down his spine; he had enough experience of war during his years of service in the army. It seemed apparent there was no alternative way of getting to the town of Misakev, and having travelled this far, he had no intention of turning back now. The news broadcast ended and Karl turned the television off. Joseph remarked, "We are now ready to go out."

Arthur went to the bathroom to refresh himself, and joining the others they walked through the town to their favourite bar. It was now eight p.m. and most of the tables were occupied by men and women drinking and chattering; the proprietor smiled and spoke to them as they entered. Karl bought the drinks and they sat down at an empty table. Several people nodded and called out to the party as they passed by; it was quite obvious they were well-known and liked.

A man rose from his chair, bringing his beer with him and started chatting to Karl. Arthur scrutinised the customers in the bar. They were a motley crowd, but all seemed to be enjoying their evening out. Karl and his visitor were still engrossed in deep conversation; Gerda was talking to a woman on the next table, Joseph exchanged a few words in English with Arthur, who was just thinking, 'I wonder what Karl and his friend are discussing,' when the friend got up and went across the room, to where an elderly man sat smoking a pipe. After a few words he came over to their table, where an extra chair was placed for him to be seated. Looking Arthur over for a few moments, and removing his pipe from his mouth, the stranger spoke in perfect English.

"Welcome to our town. My name is of no consequence, but until my retirement I was professor of English language at the university here. My friend tells me that you are trying to reach the town of Misakev. I may be able to help you. My son is in the Red Cross, and frequently has to go into the war zone to bring out the wounded; they are the only ones the guerrillas will permit to pass through the territory. My son speaks good English. I will go now and bring him back here to meet you."

Rising, he put his pipe in his pocket and departed. Joseph bought them all another beer, and they sat talking. Within half an hour the professor returned, accompanied by a middle-aged well-built man. "This is my son," he remarked, introducing him to everyone. Taking a seat next to Arthur, he began by asking how he could be of help.

Arthur explained briefly the purpose of his visit to Misakev. The younger man listened in silence, as did his father, and when Arthur had finished, he spoke to his father. "I think we might get this English gentleman through the war zone. I have an idea. Fitted up in a Red Cross uniform, he could come along as my assistant, the main problem being he does not speak our language; the warring factions are not too happy with the news many reporters are sending out to the world press about their conflict and are very suspicious of any foreigners coming into their area. However, I will make it known that you are a deaf mute, so if you are spoken to or are questioned just look vague, and do not react in any way. I shall be leaving for the battle zone tomorrow; Karl will bring you to our depot at six a.m. We have a few spare suits, I am sure one of them will fit you well enough for you to pass, and then with luck I can get you to your destination. Once there, you will be on your own. Get out of your uniform and hide it in your case, then keep your head down. You will also need some food, there is little enough in the area, so perhaps Gerda could let you have some. I hope you are happy with these arrangements, it is the best I can think of at the moment. The next difficulty will be getting you out again, but we can discuss that on our journey tomorrow." He finished his beer, spoke to his father, and left the bar.

The professor spoke to Arthur saying he understood the reason for him coming all this way in order to carry out the wishes of a dying comrade, and one of his countrymen. "You are a very fine person, Sir. Not many would have taken all this trouble to keep a promise made during the height of a battle so many years ago. I admire you and wish you luck. Should you return safely, please come and visit me, and tell me of your adventures. Karl knows where I live." He shook hands with Arthur saying, "God go with you my son," and calling "Goodnight" to the others, he left.

As Karl and the others were busy talking, Arthur picked up the glasses and went to get more beer. He held out a handful of coins, the barman took what was necessary. He returned to his seat, and the talks continued until about ten thirty p.m., Joseph speaking a few words in English now and again to keep Arthur interested. When their last drink was finished they left for home where, on arrival, Gerda produced plates of bread and cheese and a bottle of local wine. They enjoyed the refreshment and at eleven thirty, Arthur indicated that, as he must make an early start in the morning, he would retire. He went to his room, and after having a wash he got into bed. Although very tired and relaxed after the beers he had consumed, it was some time before he could sleep. He eventually drifted into deep sleep, to be suddenly awakened by someone knocking on his bedroom door. He switched on the bedside lamp to find it was nearly five a.m.

Shouting "okay" he rose and went to the bathroom, where he hurriedly shaved, washed and packed his gear back into his case. Going to the dining room, he found Gerda there in her housecoat with breakfast ready for him and Karl. A box tied with string was on the table. She and her husband chatted away, whilst Arthur sat and ate his breakfast. They had finished by five thirty. Karl picked up the box and indicated it was time for them to leave for the Red Cross station. Gerda went to the door with them, and putting her arms round Arthur's neck planted a kiss on his cheek, saying something he did not understand, but he guessed it was "Farewell" or "Take care". She waved to them as they turned into the main street and both walked briskly along, as the streets were almost empty at that time of the morning. They reached the station before six o'clock, to find it a hive of activity. The professor's son Olaf was on the look out, and seeing them enter the gate he beckoned them over to his ambulance.

"Jump in the back, Arthur," he said. "There is a uniform in there that should fit you. Pack your other clothes away in your bag and hide it under the bottom stretcher." He quickly obeyed and soon emerged dressed as a Red Cross officer. The suit fitted well. Olaf was speaking to Karl, and Arthur joined them to shake hands with Karl, who smiled and gave him the same good luck wishes as everyone gave him. Arthur climbed into the passenger seat, Olaf jumped in and, starting up the ambulance, drove out of the yard and into the street.

Three other vehicles of the same type followed, going through the town and onto the main road, leaving from the opposite direction in which they had entered in Joseph's lorry the previous day. So, thought Arthur, this is the worst part. If I can get through and return here, even if I find no trace of Ivor's family, at least I *will* know that I tried. Everyone has been so kind and helpful, I only hope and pray that I am able to relate some sort of success on my return.

The convoy travelled at a steady pace towards the borders defining the troubled areas, stopping once in a small village for refreshment and to allow time for the engines to cool down as by this time, with the sun blazing down on the dusty roads, everything had become overheated. The traffic was now becoming sparse; a farm cart or two, an occasional car loaded with goods, and groups of people going in the opposite direction. These, Arthur thought, might be travelling to get away from the hostilities further afield. Leaving the village behind, they traversed a few more miles, when the road was completely blocked by a large farm cart, loaded with household goods, a great many of which had fallen off onto the road. A wheel had come off the cart, which was now surrounded by adults and children all shouting at the top of their voices, apparently refugees escaping from the war. The horse had been removed from the shafts, and led to safety at the side of the road.

The convoy of ambulances stopped to give what help they could. An elderly man approached the first driver, and spoke rapidly to him. Picking up his first aid kit he went quickly to the other side of the road. Arthur followed and found a girl of ten or eleven years, lying on an old coat bleeding from a large gash across her head. Someone had tried to stop the bleeding with a towel but without success, while other members of the Red Cross were helping to unload the cart, so that the wheel could be fixed, whilst an elderly ambulance man was handing round mugs of water. Examining the child, Olaf turned to Arthur saying, "Please bring me a stretcher, this wound needs stitching." Arthur brought the stretcher, and they gently lifted the child onto it and carried her over to the ambulance. Carefully cutting the hair from around the wound, he asked Arthur to light the burner and to boil the water for sterilising the instruments. Taking from his bag what was required, he produced a bottle of antiseptic lotion. He poured some into the boiling water, and washed his hands in the solution. Picking up a spray, he sprayed it all over the wound. Threading a needle, he spoke soothingly to the child as he proceeded to draw the torn flesh together. The little face looked pale and frightened, but the spray must have frozen the flesh as she made no murmur during the stitching, and when it was completed Arthur handed him a sterile dressing, which he placed carefully over the wound and then bandaged it. He then gave her a tablet with a drop of water to swallow. She stirred as he cleaned the dried blood from her face, and placing a hand gently on her, he spoke. She lay back and closed her eyes.

"We will leave her here for a while, until the road is cleared, she is all right for now." They crossed the road to find the owner who, with help from the others, had the cart jacked up and the wheel, which was not too badly damaged, was being replaced. Olaf spoke to the women sitting at the roadside. One of them came over. He handed her some dressings with instructions on how to use them, explaining the condition of her daughter, with regrets that he had been unable to do anything regarding her bloodstained clothing. He looked the other children over, all of whom seemed to be very frightened but unharmed. After chatting for some time to the men repairing the cart, he joined Arthur and together they went back to their vehicle. The little girl was still sleeping peacefully, and the natural colour was returning to her face.

"She should be all right now," he remarked. "Let's see what progress they are making with clearing the road. They found that, with a united effort, the wheel and all the items that had fallen off had been replaced and the road was clear again. He spoke a few words to the mother of the injured child, who followed him to the ambulance, picked up her daughter, and carried her back to the cart where she placed her on a rug, on the floor of it.

Putting the horse back between the shafts they carefully manoeuvred past the ambulance convoy, waving and shouting what Arthur presumed to be their thanks and goodbyes. When the pathetic little party of refugees were out of ear shot, Olaf called all his men together and spoke to them at some length. It was obvious from the look on their faces that what he was telling them was not good news, and when he had finished, he turned to Arthur explaining what had been said to his party.

"Things are not so good further along," he said. "The refugees we have just helped have provided me with some up to date news of the fighting. A party of Guerrillas raided their farm last night killing all the cattle for food. They then ransacked the farm and drove them out, and another two families from nearby houses. They have taken all the buildings over as strongholds. The families were lucky to escape when they did. There is quite a battle raging now around that area which controls the adjoining points of a crossroads, so it would appear that we shall have some difficulty in getting past them. We need to go through that road to get to the temporary field hospital to pick up the seriously wounded and get them back for treatment in the city hospital. It is going to be rather hectic and frightening. My men are used to these conditions; we have been in and out of this area for some months now, and are known to the leaders of both sides. They usually allow us free passage, but sometimes an upstart of an officer, or NCO, who thinks he is running the war, makes things pretty rough for us. We have to accept that there is no ceasefire whilst we are travelling through the war zone, so it can be very dangerous. Three of our men have already been killed and two wounded over the last few weeks."

Looking at Olaf, Arthur remarked, "Don't worry about me. I served all through World War Two, so have had a lot of experience of fighting and looking after myself under gunfire. It's my guess we can take all this lot can throw at us."

"Good," said Olaf. "Then let's get started. We must try and get to the foothills of those mountains you can see ahead before it gets dark. We make camp there, have something to eat, check the vehicles, and get some sleep. We shall then be ready to try our luck at getting to the base field hospital tomorrow. An early start is necessary, so we set off at first light of early dawn. The guerrillas are less active at that time, and we might stand a better chance of getting through without facing too much shot and shell."

The convoy reached the camp site just as the sun was going down. It was obvious from the marks where fires had previously been lit before on the rough ground that the convoy had used this site before. They parked the vehicles and, to Arthur's surprise, began to collect pieces of dry wood, preparing to light a fire.

"Do you think it wise to have a fire so close to the enemy?" he enquired. "It may attract their attention to us."

"Don't worry," he was told. They will realise it is us. We always use this spot for our over night stay. We are all in need of a meal and coffee."

Two of the men unloaded cooking pots and supplies from the back of their vehicle, and soon the smell of cooking meat and boiling coffee made Arthur realise how very hungry he was. When the meal was ready they sat on the rocks surrounding the camp site and tucked into the meal. When all had finished, Olaf said:

"Let's put the fire out and clean up. We can then sleep on the stretchers in the ambulances. But there is one thing we must do, Arthur, and that is mount a guard throughout the night, taking it in turns. This is a necessity as the warring factions are not amiss at raiding our supplies, taking not only drugs and dressings, leaving us with nothing to treat the wounded, but also food for ourselves, so each of us will take an hour on duty in turn and that, I regret to say, includes you."

Whilst explaining this, he was busy writing numbers on pieces of paper and placing them in his hat. He held out the hat, saying, "Please draw these one at a time, Arthur." Dipping his hand into the hat he drew out a number. Olaf looked at the list in his hand, jotting the numbers down until the hat was empty; looking up from his task, he remarked, "Your duty is number four. We start at eight o'clock when it is quite dark, so you will be on duty from midnight. The man then on duty will wake you in good time, and then you will wake the man who is to follow you. He sleeps in number three ambulance on the stretcher at the right hand side. You can then fall in for sleep again."

Chapter Nine

"Oh! by the way, you will be armed. We have two machine pistols and plenty of ammunition. I know it seems strange for non-combatants to be armed but we have to protect ourselves and our supplies. If you see or hear anything at all suspicious whilst on duty, shout and, if need be, let off a few shots. We shall soon be at your side with the other pistol. We are in a position where it is best to shoot first and question afterwards so try to be on the alert all the time."

The camp soon settled down to sleep, with the exception of the man on duty. Arthur found that his mind was too alert for sleep; he tossed and turned on the hard stretcher, wondering what lay ahead, but nature took over and after a long and tiring day he fell asleep to be awakened soon afterwards by the man he was to relieve. Wiping the sleep from his eyes he stretched, took the pistol from the man, checked to see it was still loaded, nodded to him, and went over to sit on the large rock near to the camp, from where they had a good view of the surrounding countryside. The moon was well up by now, and cast shadows from the bushes and rocks, giving the place an eerie look. Except for the stealthy movements of night prowling animals, and the occasional call of a bird, the place was silent. Arthur settled down behind the rock and, for some considerable time, took stock of his situation. What lay ahead for tomorrow? Would the convoy get through without too many problems? What were his chances of getting to the town of Misakev, his ultimate destination? And what were his chances of getting out of this troubled area after he completed his mission there? After a time he shrugged his shoulders and, arising from the rock, he quietly walked round the camp. Suddenly from somewhere not too far distant came a loud screech, which sounded like someone in pain. He froze, cocked his pistol and held his breath. The cry was answered further up the valley. Arthur let out his breath as he realised it was only a night owl calling to its mate. His hour soon passed and, going over to ambulance three, he woke his relief, handing the pistol to him. He returned to his own stretcher, lay down and was soon asleep. He was awakened by the sound of voices and the smell of wood smoke; leaving the vehicle he saw that everyone was already up, coffee was brewing on the fire, and they all sat around eating bread and cheese.

"Goats' cheese," Olaf remarked. Arthur did not dislike it despite the strong taste, and they each drank two or three cups of coffee. They then doused the fire, cleaned up and one by one disappeared into the undergrowth taking a towel. Arthur followed and they arrived at a spring of clear water running from a crevice in the rocks. They all stripped to the waist, washed and shaved, then filled up their water containers, dressed themselves and returned to their vehicles.

"We are now about to start on the most difficult part of our journey," Olaf remarked. "If we get through the pass you can see up ahead, and on to the savanna beyond, we should have plain sailing to our Field Hospital. But it is in this pass that we are likely to meet snipers and small parties of guerrillas, so let's get started and try to keep our heads down, hoping that things will be quiet for a change."

Starting the motors the party moved out onto the road, on their way towards the pass. As they neared it Arthur experienced a cold prickly sensation down the back of his neck, the like of which he had not felt since going into battle during the last war. 'Old habits die hard,' he thought. 'I am sure I can still cope under fire, but let's hope we can get through without any problems.'

The convoy made good time towards the pass. Once or twice they came across a party of refugees going in the opposite direction. Olaf stopped to talk to one party of about twenty men, women and children and discovered they had been subjected to heavy bombardment; their homes destroyed and some of their families killed when the buildings collapsed. They were making their way from the war zone, hoping to find help and shelter in the nearest large town. It would appear from what they said that the fighting was intensifying in the area they were now approaching. They pressed on and by midday pulled up at the road side for a meal. As the noise of their engines receded, the sound of heavy shelling could be heard in the distance. Olaf remarked, "It looks as if we shall have to run the gauntlet through the pass. Should it be too bad, I will decide what is best to do. We either wait until the battle quietens down, or make the return journey home. I have no wish to subject my men and vehicles to unnecessary danger. A decision will be made when we reach the pass."

Realising how important the journey was to Arthur, he looked at him saying, "Don't worry, we might still be able to get you through to Misakev." They cleared up and started on their way, the pass getting ever nearer and the sound of gunfire louder and more sustained with each mile they travelled. At the entrance to the pass, which they reached just after five o'clock, Olaf halted the convoy and took stock of the situation ahead. It was apparent that the two warring factions were shelling each other across the pass. Each side had set up opposing positions and were firing into the mountains; some of the shells were dropping on to the lower parts of the mountain, posing a threat to anyone going along the narrow road. They watched as shells burst uncomfortably near, throwing pieces of shrapnel and rock far and wide.

"We will wait here," Olaf decided. "I will go forward under the Red Cross flag, and hope to attract the attention of one of the officers. Perhaps I can persuade them to cease shelling whilst we pass through. It is only a matter of ten or twelve kilometres and we could then travel more safely."

Fetching the flag from the rear of the ambulance he unfurled it and, raising it above his head, went forward up the pass. At that particular part it was safe from shell fire. They watched with apprehension as he made his way along and disappeared out of sight, round a bend.

They waited with bated breath for his return. Two of the men lit a fire and brewed the usual billy of coffee; it was an excuse to have something to occupy their minds, and the coffee was most welcome. They stood around, listening to the battle raging ahead, waiting; nerves were taut and cigarettes were being lit one after another to help keep them calm. Olaf had been gone nearly an hour and dusk was beginning to fall when he appeared round the bend in the road. The battle seemed to be intensifying and, to those waiting, it appeared from his dejected manner he had met with little success. Reaching the party he sat down wearily on a rock and was handed a cup of coffee, which he sipped, meanwhile brushing some of the dust from his uniform. He spoke at some length to his men, then turned to Arthur explaining what he had just told the men.

"I managed to talk to a commander from each of the warring

factions. They came down to the road to speak to me, respecting my flag. Although they realise that we are non-combatant, and both sides have badly wounded men needing to be removed to hospital," he hesitated, "they are not prepared to cease firing to allow us through the pass. It seems that this battle is to win and hold this pass, and whoever is the winner will be able to control all supplies passing along this road, which is the only way through for food and ammunition, and they will fight to the bitter end to hold it. They did say, however, that they can try to keep any shells falling short and landing on the lower slopes and the road but admit their gunnery is not very accurate, so I suggest we wait until dark, and make a run for it, keeping our fingers crossed that the gunners up there in the mountains are more accurate at hitting their enemies than us. We might as well get some rest, and try our luck about midnight, Perhaps by then they will all be fed up and tired and leave off shelling until morning. By that time we should be clear of the pass, and well on the way to our field hospital."

The men agreed to this with a nod of the head, and settled down in the ambulances for an hour or two's rest, keeping a wary eye out still for anyone who might be up to no good. Arthur sat on the rear step of his vehicle with the machine pistol across his knees, checking that it was loaded. He relaxed, and thought, 'How like old times, with nerves set taut, and adrenaline flowing just waiting to go into battle.'

The moon was obscured by low clouds, he checked his watch by the dim light. Two hours to go and the sound of guns echoed down the pass. 'They sound like howitzers,' he thought. 'How in the hell had they got heavy artillery like that up the sides of these forbidding mountains? Well,' he realised, 'we had done the same thing by sheer brute strength and willpower in many parts of the world during the last war, so perhaps that is how these people managed it.'

He was drifting into sleep when he was awakened by a shell landing uncomfortably near, close enough to cause particles of shrapnel and stones to rattle on the roofs of the vehicles. This woke the others who came out to see what was happening. "Now why should they fire in this direction," remarked Olaf, "when the actual fighting is nearly three miles up the road."

"Perhaps", answered Arthur, "they are firing at a party of the enemy trying to get down from the mountain, cross the road in the darkness, slip in behind at the other side, and attack from the rear."

Olaf jumped up, "That is possible, and if so, that means that an armed party could be quite near. We must be on the alert as they might mistake us for a hostile band and attack us. Quickly," he called to his men, "Cut some of the bushes and try to camouflage our vehicles.

"No," shouted Arthur. "That would make it look most suspicious. The best thing to do is to light a fire so our Red Cross Ambulances can be seen. As a precaution, two of us can take cover with the pistols, and if any hostility is shown towards us, we are in a position to defend ourselves."

Olaf replied, "We will do that," and explained this to his men, who quickly lit a fire.

One of the men joined Arthur behind some rocks, facing up the pass, armed with the other pistol. They did not have long to wait; in the moonlight, they discerned a party of some thirty or more men moving cautiously down towards the road trying to keep in the shadows thrown by the boulders.

The shelling overhead had slackened off a little. Arthur and his companion kept careful watch on the approaching men. One must have spotted the fire and pointed his rifle toward the vehicles. They advanced nearer to the camp with extreme caution until, within a few hundred metres, they must have realised the vehicles were ambulances, for one of them came forward waving a piece of white material, his rifle held well above his head. Olaf went to meet him in No Man's Land. They held a hurried conversation out there, then turned around and rejoined their respective parties. As soon as he arrived back, he turned to Arthur saying:

"You were quite right in your supposition; that is exactly what that party and others that we have not yet seen are doing. They hope to get round to the rear of the enemies guns, attack, and put them out of action. At least that would leave us a clear passage through." The words had hardly left his mouth when the sound of fierce machine and rifle fire erupted on the side of the hills; the party that had been within sight a few moments ago had run into an enemy contingent with the same idea in mind. The fighting became much fiercer, the guns started up in all their fury, machine guns were hammering out the death knell for many, and tracer bullets were flying in all directions. The screams and cries of the wounded could be heard above the terrible sound of the raging battle.

Arthur looked around. The men were all flat upon the ground. A stray bullet had hit the windscreen of one of the vehicles, showering glass over a wide area. Another hit the side of the next ambulance, so it was wise to keep one's head down, but he still kept a cautious eye on what was happening on the hillside. A man suddenly appeared in front of him swaying from side to side. As he came nearer Arthur could see he was unarmed, and blood was flowing freely down his right arm. He collapsed in front of the rock behind which Arthur had taken cover; he was badly in need of help. Arthur rose at the same time as Olaf. They moved forward and together lifted the wounded man and carried him to their ambulance.

"Leave this to me," Olaf remarked. "I will take care of him. You take cover again." The battle seemed to be getting even worse, then suddenly the shooting stopped. Arthur could see men running back over the road towards the positions from which they had come; the silence was intense after such a fierce exchange of fire. Remaining where he was for a time, Arthur heard Olaf calling him.

"This is the man I spoke to earlier on. From what he tells me his party has been ambushed by the opposing side, and there are many men up there, either dead or wounded. As soon as it is light enough to climb the rocks, we must try and tend the wounded; that is all we can do."

Looking upward to the sky, Arthur saw a glimmer of light over to the East and remarked, "It should be light enough to risk a climb, in about half an hour or so."

The men set to, filling their satchels with dressings and antiseptics, then unstrapping the stretchers from the vehicles. They were well trained, having faced similar situations during previous tours of duty; they knew what needed to be done. Two men, with the pistols, would have to be left behind to safeguard the camp and the ambulances. The party set off as soon as dawn broke, climbing the rough terrain with some trepidation. The going was treacherous, and within minutes they came upon the carnage left by the recent battle: bodies of men lay about like broken dolls, many obviously dead, others very badly wounded. The party were soon at work sterilising and bandaging wounds, attending first to the ones who needed urgent treatment, and getting them down to the waiting ambulances. Two of the soldiers succumbed to their wounds before help reached them.

Arthur and Olaf were attending to a young soldier who had been wounded in the thigh; the flesh and muscle were badly torn, and he was bleeding profusely. They applied a tourniquet, and whilst they were putting on the dressing they realised they were, at the moment, completely alone in the battle area, the others having gone back down to the road, bearing the stretcher cases. They had been too busy to notice that four of the opposing enemy had silently crept up on them, and were pointing their guns at the backs of Olaf and Arthur. The wounded man they were attending to saw the soldiers approaching. Arthur saw the fear in his eyes as he cried out to warn them; Olaf turned and then continued to apply the dressing to the wound.

One of the four came closer. 'An officer,' thought Arthur as he stood beside them and shouted something Arthur didn't understand. Olaf completed the dressing before rising and putting his hands above his head, indicating to Arthur to do the same, endeavouring to let him know that these were the men who had ambushed the ones they were helping. The officer made a threatening motion with his gun, and called the others over. Coming forward, one produced a rope from his pocket and grasping Arthur's hands, he pulled them down and tied them securely behind his back, then proceeded to do the same with Olaf, who was angrily remonstrating with the officer who, making no reply, went among the bodies lying on the ground moving each one with his foot. He must have realised that all but the one they had been treating were dead. Muttering something to his men, two of them picked up the wounded man who let out a scream of agony, but they took no notice.

The officer again threatened them with his gun, then herded them upwards over the rocks and along a very narrow pathway. The party went stumbling and struggling over the rough ground. Olaf had tried several times to converse with the officer but had been ignored. At a very difficult part of the track, when the attention of the men was occupied trying to negotiate an awkward corner, he turned to Arthur and mouthed, "Don't speak in English." He silently nodded to show he understood, and the party continued upwards towards their positions on the mountainside.

The wounded soldier was by now unconscious. Blood was seeping through the dressing, his face was grey from loss of blood, and he urgently needed a blood transfusion.

After about another half hour's journey they were challenged by a sentry some few metres away. The party stopped, the officer went forward, then beckoned the others to follow, and they entered a gun position. Although the men were resting, Arthur noticed that they had guns in position behind large boulders with binoculars trained over the pass on the opposing guns. It was apparent they were keeping a careful watch on the enemy. The men carrying the wounded soldier set him down on the ground; one spoke to Olaf who immediately sat down, so Arthur followed suit, he then realised that one of the party had brought along Olaf's medical bag which had been placed beside them. A soldier remained with them, as a guard it would seem; the other went to speak to a man in camouflage uniform – from the green tags on his collar and the gold stars on each patch, probably the commanding officer of the battery. They talked for some considerable time, and the man guarding the wounded soldier, walked away to get a light for his cigarette from one of his comrades. This gave Olaf the chance to whisper to Arthur, "Don't for God's sake say anything. I have told them you are a deaf mute. They have brought us here in order that we can treat some of the wounded they have brought back from the battlefield. I think they have also brought this young soldier, to question him as to the strength of the enemy on the other side of the mountain, where his party came from. Keep perfectly still, and don't move, even if the guns restart, as that will give the game away. I only hope our other members managed to escape, and are getting the wounded into hospital. I wonder if they will realise and report our capture."

He stopped talking as the guard returned with the senior officer who came forward and ordered the guard to release their hands. Telling them to stand he led them away from the wounded man to a small clearing behind the gun emplacements, where they found eight men lying with varying types of wounds needing immediate attention. He spoke again and handed the medical bag to Olaf, leaving them to get on with the treatment. Olaf called him back and spoke to him. The officer nodded and turned away and a few moments later a man came over carrying a large bucket of water. They both set to work tending the wounded, making them as comfortable as was possible; some needed more help than they were able to provide, but they did what they could for each one.

After having been busy for more than an hour one of the gunners came over and placed two mugs of coffee, and some bread and cheese on a nearby rock. At least, thought Arthur, they don't intend to starve us.

Just as they were finishing with the wounded the soldier they had carried from the bottom of the mountain was brought in. He was still unconscious, his wounds still bleeding badly. One of the stretcher bearers spoke, then left them. After changing his dressing, they forced a little water into his mouth and made him as comfortable as they could.

"He needs a blood transfusion urgently," Olaf muttered in his ear, "but that is impossible up here. Without it he will die before morning."

Moving apart from the wounded, they sat down to drink the coffee and eat the food provided. This gave Olaf a chance to speak again to Arthur.

"We are in a bit of a mess. They have no intention of freeing us, and they are expecting this man back well enough to answer their questions. I don't think that will be possible, so we shall have to watch our step."

Soon after they had eaten twilight began to fall, so the dressings all had to be attended to again, before it became too dark to see. Going over to check the young soldier, they were amazed to find him conscious. Olaf spoke to him for a few moments, then took some papers from his battle dress pocket and read them in the fading light, and with a look of incredulity on his face, turned to Arthur, and remarked, "What did you say, was the name of the family, you have come so far to find?" He looked at Arthur expectantly. "Kaldev," replied Arthur. "Why?"

"Well, you will hardly believe it, but that is the name of this young man," and he handed the soldier's documents to Arthur who, in what little light that was left, managed to read them.

Yes, the soldier's name was Kaldev, Hugo Kaldev number 2437819, born in the town of Misakev. Was this really one of his old friend's relatives? "Is he well enough to answer any questions?" he asked. "Where is Misakev? Does he live there? Are there any more of the same name living in the town? Is the town still standing, and can I get into it?"

"Steady," Olaf replied. "I will talk quietly to him. We must not tire him too much," and with that, Arthur had to be content. His excitement grew with each passing moment as Olaf spoke quietly to the wounded man, who was answering in a very weak voice, stopping now and then when Olaf gave him sips of water. Arthur did not dare

to ask for an explanation of the conversation lest he broke their train
of thought.

The young soldier started to speak again. Olaf had to put his ear
close up to his mouth in an effort to catch the words, his voice
becoming weaker as his life ebbed away; they spoke to each other for
a minute or two, Olaf nodding his head occasionally then, giving him
another sip of water, he tried by lifting his head up a little to make
him more comfortable. Looking around Arthur saw in the distance
the CO approaching them. He touched Olaf on the shoulder and
whispered to him. He ceased talking to the soldier and began
adjusting the man's dressings, at the same time putting a finger over
his lips, indicating that Arthur should not speak or move, so he
pretended to be asleep.

Reaching Olaf the officer knelt down and spoke to him. He shook
his head, showing the officer the blood soaked dressing. Arthur did
not know what was said, but the officer got up and walked away again
looking very angry, evidently annoyed that he was unable to
interrogate the wounded man. When all was quiet, Arthur whispered
to Olaf, "Did you discover anything from this poor young man that
might help in my quest to find Ivor's relatives?"

"Yes and no," Olaf replied. "As I said before, his name is Hugo
Kaldev, and he lived in the town of Misakev. He was conscripted into
the rebel army just over a year ago, and has not been home since. He
has a father, mother, and two sisters who, as far as he knows, are still
safe and living in their home. Despite the fact that part of the town
has been damaged during the war, he recalls that there is an elderly
relative living in the town, but in what part she lives, or what her
name is he does not know. She may be the sister of Ivor. There is
little I can do for him now, he has lost so much blood, but if he should
rally and be able to talk again, I will try and get more information
from him. I don't hold out much hope of that."

"What did the officer want?" asked Arthur.

"Oh! He wanted to know if the soldier was able to talk. He
needed to question him as to the strength of the battery on the other
side of the pass, and what Infantry was in support. I told him it was
unlikely that he would regain consciousness, and that his wounds were
so bad it would be a miracle if he survived until sunrise. He was very
angry as you saw, and stamped away in a rage. What a good thing he
didn't come whilst Hugo was talking, or he would have been

interrogated regardless of his condition, and it would have served little purpose. War is so cruel."

With that he lay down and closed his eyes, but there was to be no sleep for any of them tonight.

Suddenly and without any warning a battery of guns from the opposing side opened up with a terrific salvo. Arthur could make no guess as to the amount of guns used, but they must all have been fired together. Shells landed around them in all directions sending up fountains of earth and rock, some dropping in close proximity as they huddled up tight in the shelter of the boulders. Turning to the wounded man Olaf felt his pulse and over the roar of exploding shells called out, "We shall not get anything more from this brave young man, he is already dead."

It was at this moment that the guns beside them went into action, and from then on conversation was impossible. The battle raged across the pass for more than two hours. Their position was hit by a number of heavy shells, and wounded men were brought over for Olaf to treat, but his medical supplies were almost exhausted so there was little he could now do.

Chapter Ten

The guns opposite seemed to have got the range of their position, as more and more shells were reaching their target. One must have hit an ammunition store, for the ground heaved and shook whilst the blast deafened them. Three soldiers, one a sergeant, appeared before them, shouting and pointing rifles at them:

"We are leaving, and must go with these men."

The soldiers were too shocked to hear what Arthur was being told; they were in a hurry to leave. Others joined the party with several officers who were helping to lay fuses along the ground. Retreat in disarray was obvious, and from what they were about to do, nothing would be left for the enemy to claim as spoils of war. They were to be hurried over the other side of the mountain, away from the opposing side. An officer who had run out a fuse knelt down and lit it from his cigarette lighter, shouting to his men as he hurried forward. They picked up speed, stumbling over the rough ground, and reached a flat area covered at intervals with large boulders of rocks, behind which they hastily took cover, just as an explosive roar rent the air, and huge flames erupted into the sky, throwing up pieces of metal and rocks from the place they had been standing on only a few minutes before. The whole battery had disappeared in a column of flame and smoke. It was only then that Arthur realised that the wounded lying near them in the gun emplacement had not been brought out; in their haste to escape from the terrible shelling, a retreat had been made without thought of their wounded comrades.

The sound of explosions still echoed round the mountainside. The officers took charge, shouting orders to the men who, with as much speed as was possible over this rough terrain, made their way down the other side of the mountain. After more than an hour's journey they reached the plains to find hidden in a gully a number of army vehicles being guarded by a few armed men. Seeing the approaching soldiers the guards hurried forward, exchanging a few words with an officer, and every one hastily mounted the vehicles and went racing across the plain; not too soon, for some of the enemy had already reached the place where the trucks had been, and were firing machine guns in their direction. They were too far away to do any damage to the convoy which was travelling pretty fast, proving to be a dusty and bumpy ride. Trying to estimate the number of men left, Arthur thought there could only be ninety to one hundred, so half of the battery must have been lost, plus all the guns and ammunition. The trucks rolled over the parched ground, leaving thick clouds of dust in their wake, for more than two hours.

'Whenever are we going to stop?' thought Arthur.

He dared not speak to Olaf, for the armed guard was watching them intently. They evidently had orders to keep a careful eye on their captives. "What the devil are they going to do with us? Of what value are two Red Cross men to such rabble as this?" he thought.

He and Olaf were soon to know the answer to that question. Suddenly the vehicle came to a halt. Both were dragged out of the truck by armed men. Wiping the dust from his eyes, Arthur saw that they were standing before a large mansion. The men got out and, falling into line, marched away to the rear of the house. An officer came forward and spoke to Olaf and, with guards, they were taken up the steps and into the house, being called to a halt just inside the large entrance hall, the guards menacing them with guns. The officer knocked on a door and entered the room. Coming out a few moments later he barked an order to the guards who jabbed their rifles into the backs of the two men and marched them into the room. They were followed by the officer closing the door and saluting the man seated at a desk and facing them. He appeared to be an officer of high rank by the amount of gold braid adorning his uniform. He returned the salute and stood up, the better to examine his prisoners (for that is what they were), sat down again, lit a cigarette and spoke to them in his own language. "Well, well, what have we here? Two Red Cross men guilty of spying for the enemy."

Olaf erupted. Words of protest came tumbling from him, and Arthur watched him getting red in the face with anger. The officer let him go on for some moments, then held up his hand to silence him, and to Arthur's surprise spoke in perfect English.

"Let's speak in your comrade's tongue," he said. "Yes, we know he is an Englishman, sent to spy on us by the other side. Why is he masquerading in a non-combatant uniform in a foreign country, with a convoy of ambulances, accompanied by a genuine Red Cross officer?"

The two men were stunned into silence by these accusations. The officer continued, "We are holding you as our prisoners, and will interrogate you both in due course. We intend to discover what you have found out about our defences and deployment of our troops, which you have been conveying to our enemy."

Reverting to his own language he spoke to the officer and guards, "Take them away and lock them up with the other prisoners."

They were marched out, round the rear of the house, past the tents of the soldiers, to a barbed wire cage, in which thirty or forty men were milling around. There was no shelter, no room to sit down, there were no toilet facilities, and the fenced-in area was very small. A guard at the gate to the prison camp opened it and the two were bundled in. The gate was slammed shut, and barred behind them. Some of the men came forward and spoke to Olaf. They also fired questions at Arthur but, not understanding, he shook his head, pointing to his mouth and ears. They must have realised he did not know their language. After some time they drifted away, leaving the two alone. Olaf then told Arthur a little of the talks they had been having, and how concerned they were about the battle on the mountain and the loss of their many comrades.

"This is the third set back they have suffered in the last few weeks. They are all becoming very depressed, feeling that they are losing the war. Food is so scarce, they are only being given one poor meal a day, with a mug of water to drink. Sanitation is non-existent and some are already suffering from diarrhoea and are in need of treatment. we look to be in dire trouble here."

"Yes," replied Arthur. "We are certainly in a bad situation. Apart from the fact that they seem convinced that I am a spy, there also appears to be doubt as to your intentions. This prison camp is the worst I have ever seen, and I saw a few in the last war. I was held in one for a few months, until we escaped.

"Escaped?" Olaf gasped. "How did you manage that?"

"We watched and waited, made our plans accordingly and took our chance when we thought time was in our favour, and we got away with it and back to our own lines again. Only three of us were involved; any more would have made it impossible. We kept our plans to ourselves, and made the break without letting any of the others into our secret."

Olaf was silent for a moment then, turning to Arthur, asked, "What do you think of our chances of getting out of here?"

Arthur considered the question for a while, saying, "Let's walk about, have a good look round, and see what the lie of the land is, but we must not make it too obvious." They strolled around the camp, stopping to speak to one or two prisoners occasionally and taking in everything they saw.

The first impression was that the camp looked a bit rough and ready, but on closer inspection it proved to be better guarded than they thought, and the fence was not as temporary as it appeared. A mesh fence had been erected about four metres high, topped with razor wire; beyond that lay a patch of no man's land of about five or six metres, then another fence of barbed wire, closely woven, and about the same height as the first one. Arthur looked carefully at the fences, and then at the ground between them.

"I suspect there are booby trap mines set in amidst the two fences, with hidden trip wires to contend with as well. The guards are not too much of a problem, they seem content to stand about smoking, feeling no doubt that the two fences with the mines buried beneath are sufficient to deter anyone from trying to get out. There doesn't seem to be any flood lighting for use after dark, so night time is going to be our best bet. We will play it by ear for the time being, and see what transpires."

They sat down together on the dusty floor to discuss the situation. Looking up they saw the officer approaching, followed by ten armed soldiers and a small van. The gates were opened to allow them all to enter, then swung to again and locked. A sergeant barked out an order, and the prisoners shuffled into some sort of formation. "Food time," Olaf remarked. "Let's line up. We must eat whatever we can get to keep up our strength," and they joined the queue.

On reaching the van they were handed two thick slices of coarse bread, with a hunk of cheese between, and a mug of weak coffee. The man serving said 'Keep the mugs, they are yours." Moving a little away from the others they sat down to eat their food. Some of the prisoners sat leaning back on the fence, looking pale and unsure as to whether to eat their food.

A sergeant joined them and Olaf asked him why the men were not eating their food. "They have stomach trouble, due to poor sanitary conditions, and if flies touch the food they spread the disease."

Arthur and Olaf looked at the food they held and seeing it was free from flies ate it quickly, washing it down with the coffee. Olaf and the NCO had quite a long chat, after which the NCO got up and left. Olaf then related to Arthur what had been said.

"He and several of his men were captured about three weeks ago, in a battle not far from the village you are making for. It has suffered from a lot of shelling, and most of the population have fled into the hills to avoid capture, but his pocket of troops were overrun by the enemy, brought here, interrogated, then thrown into this POW camp, and nothing has been done since. Two men tried to escape a few nights ago but were shot dead, so that has deterred anyone else from trying."

"Did you tell him we were planning to escape?" asked Arthur.

"Oh! no," Olaf replied. "You advised me to keep it a secret between us."

"We stand a much better chance of getting out on our own," replied Arthur. "If anyone finds out what we intend to do they will want to come with us and that would be a disaster. Let's find somewhere to lie down and sleep."

They settled in a corner of the fence where they could lean back, and sat in silence. Dusk was falling as the sun slowly set and a cooling breeze had sprung up freshening the air a little.

Olaf was looking across the compound toward the horizon. He nudged Arthur's arm. "Look," he pointed to where the sun was setting. "That, if I am not mistaken, is a storm brewing and from the feel of the wind, it is coming in our direction." Arthur looked to where he was pointing and, sure enough, dark thundery clouds were piling up in the sky. As they gazed a far distant flash of lightning lit up the black clouds. The thunder which must have followed it was too far away to be heard. All around the camp prisoners were settling down on the bare earth, trying to make themselves comfortable enough to get some sleep, and it was not long before the sound of thunder in the distance could be heard. Some of the men fell asleep; others looked with some apprehension at the heavy clouds becoming more visible with every flash of lightning, but they remained where they were. Where else was there to go? The storm was getting nearer.

The moon was rising behind the thunder clouds, giving the edges a silver outline, and although the compound was still dry the storm was rapidly advancing in their direction. When overhead, it suddenly burst in all its fury, and the rain deluged down, turning the dry ground into mud within minutes. The lightning seemed incessant, and the roaring thunder shook the ground beneath them. The men hardly turned a hair. With nowhere to go they lay there in the mud, deafened by the thunder and battered by the torrential rain. Arthur and Olaf were saturated in no time. Getting up from the ground, they walked a few metres away from the fence to let the rain drip off them, then stopped to wipe the rain from their faces, when a mighty flash of lightning knocked them flat on their faces, momentarily stunning them. A loud clap of thunder followed leaving them dazed and deafened. Raising his head Arthur looked around and could hardly believe what he saw. Both fences had gone and a large hole had been blown in the ground between them. In a flash he realised that here was their chance of escape. Digging his elbow into Olaf's side he pulled him round and in the light of another flash of lightning he also saw the gap. Without hesitation they ran through, half expecting to hear a burst of machine gun fire. When nothing happened, they looked back after clearing the camp, and in the dim light could see others running away. They could only think that the guards had taken refuge in the nearby building which seemed to be the guard house, not expecting anything untoward to happen, whilst the storm was still raging. Two other prisoners caught up with them. One was the sergeant they had previously spoken to who, over the din of the storm, shouted something to Olaf and pointed to his right. "He is trying to reach the road and perhaps find a vehicle. If we wish we can go along with them."

The party of four made a hurried scramble over the soaking ground, slipping and falling occasionally. Although the storm was by now abating, clouds were covering the moon which made finding their way difficult. They had to rely on flashes of lightning from the storm. Ahead of them in the dim light could be seen a darker form on the horizon. Coming closer this proved to be a large clump of trees, under which they took cover. The chatter of machine gun fire could now be heard from far away in the distance. As the storm receded, the guards must have discovered the prisoners had all escaped, and were perhaps shooting at shadows.

"We must hurry," said Olaf. "They have discovered our escape, and will be setting out to find us without delay."

The sergeant who was leading them suddenly stopped and, crouching behind a tree, signalled the party to do the same. He whispered something to Olaf, and leaving them behind the tree cautiously crept forward, and within moments was out of sight. It was very dark inside the wood, and after about five minutes he came back quietly, holding his fingers to his lips, and leaned forward to whisper in their ears.

Olaf quickly translated. "Some of the enemy are hidden in the woods here with transport close by. He thinks he can divert their attention whilst I steal a truck." They held another whispered conference, and then explained their intentions to Arthur.

"There are only about six men guarding the vehicles. The sergeant will get round to the other side and cause a commotion, whilst we go into the vehicle park taking the first one we can get started. The road is straight up ahead. He will try and join us there. If there is time, he wants us to try and sabotage some of the other vehicles. We shall have to think of a way to do so when we see what type they are."

The sergeant moved quietly away, and when he had disappeared into the darkness, they crept stealthily towards the place indicated where the vehicles were likely to be. Reaching the clearing they hid behind some bushes and waited. They could see two or three men smoking and moving around the seven vehicles parked in a line one behind the other and facing the road in readiness for moving out when needed. The track on which they were standing was narrow, with large mature trees on each side. 'Aha!' thought Arthur, 'If we can secure the first one, and disable the next in line they will be unable to move without cutting down the trees, and that would take up valuable time.'

Just then they heard shouting and screaming from afar, and the men guarding the vehicles ran towards the sound. Two jumped from the cab of the first vehicle and followed their comrades, going to investigate the commotion going on at the other side of the clearing.

Arthur and his party heard lots of shouting, and then some shots rang out. Reaching the first vehicle in the line, the one from which the two guards had jumped, Arthur opened the door of the cab and, peering in, found the keys still in the ignition with the engine still warm. Evidently the two soldiers had been running the engine to keep warm. He jumped in and the others climbed in the rear. It started at the first turn of the key, so putting it into gear he drove along the narrow track hoping the sergeant had not been wounded or captured. Behind him he could hear the guards shouting as they opened up with their rifles, and bullets rattled at the rear of the truck, but on turning a bend in the track they were well clear and there ahead stood the sergeant waving them down. He jumped onto the running board frantically waving forward, and shouting something.

Olaf then said, "There is a road up ahead. The sergeant has sabotaged the first two vehicles in the line so they cannot follow us, but they will try to get through the forest and cut us off where the track joins the road."

They sped along bumping, rattling and swaying from side to side over the rough terrain. Arthur kept the lights on in order to see any obstacles on the ground in front, but as they were travelling through thick forest they were not likely to be seen. Coming to the end of the track they encountered a crossroads.

"Which way?" shouted Arthur above the noise of the engine, as he slowed down to make a turn.

The sergeant had been clinging to the door of the cab but now managed to slide inside and commented, "Turn right or we shall be running back into enemy lines."

Once on the metalled road they made good speed, and soon left enemy territory behind. "How did the sergeant sabotage the trucks?" asked Arthur. Olaf had a short conversation with the sergeant, then turned to tell him that the fuel and brake pipes of the first two had been severed and as nothing could be moved past them on the narrow track they could not be followed. Arthur drove in desperation towards what he hoped would be comparative safety. "Does he know where we are going?" asked Arthur. Olaf spoke again to the sergeant. "Yes, he does. His own forces are reforming in the hope of beating the enemy back and reversing their defeat. They are holding a village further on, so we may find food and shelter and perhaps a way out of this mess."

Travelling a further twenty or so kilometres, they turned another bend in the road and entered the village. Arthur stopped when challenged by the sentries. It was impossible to recognise anyone in the darkness and they had no desire to be mistaken for the enemy and shot. Getting down from the cab, the sergeant spoke to the sentries, then returned to converse with the others. Olaf translated for him. "We are among friends. The men here are what is left of the sergeant's company. Get down, and we shall be given food and shelter, and can speak with the CO in the morning." A sentry moved the truck behind one of the houses.

The party were then escorted to a large house further down the street. The rooms seemed full of sleeping soldiers with a few lamps still burning. The sergeant led them through to a much larger room at the rear, apparently the dining room, in the centre of which was a long table, displaying loaves of bread, chunks of cheese, and a quantity of cold chicken pieces, whilst on top of the stove were several large jugs containing hot coffee. They found mugs, helped themselves to food and drink, and sat down to enjoy a hasty meal. When that was finished, the sergeant found them places to lay down, and after the hectic and tiring last few hours all were soon sound asleep.

They awoke to the sound of heavy boots marching around the rooms. Joining the line of men for breakfast, all were being handed a thick slice of bread and a mug of coffee. Strange looks were cast their way by some of the soldiers, who no doubt wondered what two Red Cross officers were doing among them. There was no time for explanations, as they had barely swallowed the sparse breakfast when a corporal came and asked them to accompany him. Leading them from the house, they crossed the road and entered a house opposite guarded on each side of the door by sentries. Within was a small hall, with three doors leading off. The corporal knocked on one and entered, and leaving the door open and coming out a few minutes later, he indicated they should enter the room, and followed them in.

Seated at a desk, facing them, was a portly grey-haired officer. Glancing at the party he pointed to the two chairs in front of his desk, on which Olaf and Arthur sat down and waited. He finished what he was writing in a ledger, put down his pen, and started to question them. Olaf must have explained to him that Arthur was an Englishman, for the officer nodded to him, but continued to converse with Olaf, allowing him time to translate when he had finished.

"He says he is pleased we were able to escape and he will do all that is possible to help us to return home. Meanwhile we are welcome to shelter and share their meagre rations, as it may be some days before he can get us out of here and back to the place which was our last camp site. You will, I am sure, be surprised to learn, Arthur, that this is the village you set out to reach. Yes, this is Misakev, so with luck you may be able to obtain the information you came so far to find."

It took some time for Arthur to realise his amazing good fortune. He then remarked, "Would you ask the officer if I am free to move about the village?" Olaf spoke to the officer, then turned saying,

"Yes, you are free to move around and speak to anyone. There are still many of the natives living here, depending on this army to protect them and their property."

"Will you come with me, as my interpreter?"

"Yes of course. It is unlikely any of the villagers can speak English, unless maybe the priest can."

At the mention of the priest, Arthur remembered the list Father Procovitch had given him. He consulted it and found the name of the priest was on the list. "Let's start with him. If he has lived in the village for some time he may be able to help us."

Making their way through the village towards the church they encountered soldiers everywhere. Vehicles were parked in the streets and cottage gardens, and on arrival at the church they found this also was being used to house the military. Standing beside the church was a sergeant from whom they made enquiries as to where they might find the priest. He pointed to the rear of the church, so taking the direction indicated they came to the priest's house. Before they could knock, a voice from behind spoke, and they turned to find the priest there – an elderly man with greying hair, a clear complexion and an enquiring look in his eyes.

Olaf answered him and he opened the door of his home for them, then turned to Arthur saying, "I speak some English so we can continue in your own language; it will be easier than your friend having to translate for you." He took them through to his sitting room saying, "Please sit down. I will make some coffee, then perhaps you can explain to me how, and why, an English gentleman arrives at my church, attired as a Red Cross officer, and in what way I might be of help. This is not a happy place with our people in turmoil at war, though for the moment things are quiet here. We have had fighting in and around the village with property damaged and looted. Many of the population have been killed or wounded, so we keep on the alert in case of fighting breaking out again."

He rose and left the room, returning with three mugs of coffee, on a tray.

"Now my friends, in what way can I be of help? If you are looking for a way out of here to get back to your home town, I'm afraid that right now it would be a very difficult undertaking."

"Yes and no are the answers to your questions," Olaf replied. "My English friend is on a mission in this area which he hopes to fulfil, if possible before having to return to England. He can explain this to you himself, then perhaps we can consider what steps to take to solve his problem, and then get out of the war zone. With the unhappy memories we have of the treatment meted out to us by the opposing side in this war, being accused of spying for the enemy and held as prisoners of war, we have no desire to fall into their hands again. However hear my friend's story."

Arthur retold his story whilst sipping his coffee. The priest listened with interest, nodding now and then, when the narrative ended, he remained deep in thought for some time before saying, "A very interesting story."

Arthur took the photograph from Ivor's papers, and handed it to the priest saying, "Here is a picture of Ivor's family."

Gazing at it for a while he handed it back, saying, "I recognise the cottage; it lies a little way out of the village, but I don't think the people living there now are the ones in the picture. I do not know many of the people by name as very few come to the church since the military took it over. We are only allowed to hold a short Mass once a month. As you have clearance from the officer commanding this garrison and can move freely around, I suggest you take a walk and see if there is anyone at the cottage. If they are not his people, they may know what has happened to them."

Finishing the coffee, they shook hands with the priest who gave them directions for finding the place they wanted. They left walking briskly in the direction given them. Reaching the outskirts of the village, a sentry accosted them, taking their papers and the permit from the CO. He read them through then spoke to Olaf who, as they walked away, explained to Arthur, "He warns us to be careful. The enemy sometimes carries out small sorties, trying to assess the strength of the garrison, so we must be back in the village before dark, as they double the sentry guard at sunset."

Walking in silence each was busy with his own thoughts. There were houses on both sides of the road, some of which had been damaged by shell fire, others still in good order showing signs of occupation, with washing on the lines blowing in the breeze. An elderly man tending his garden looked up in surprise as they passed, but did not speak. At the end of the road was the cottage standing apart from the village community, in its own plot of land. At first sight it appeared to be deserted and unoccupied.

Chapter Eleven

Pushing open the gate they walked along the winding path to the front entrance, where Arthur lifted the large iron knocker and gave two hard bangs on the door. As there was no response he gave it another two or three bangs. Hearing movements behind the door, they listened and heard a woman's voice trembling with fear call out. Olaf translated. She is asking "Who is there?'" He spoke at some length to the woman.

"I have told her we are friends and wish to speak to her." She spoke again and Olaf answered. This he repeated to Arthur.

"She is suspicious of us, so I have told her to look at us from the window to ensure we are not the military."

The curtain of the front window moved aside, and a few minutes later the bolts of the door were being drawn. The door creaked open and in the gloom of the hallway stood a tall grey-haired woman. She stood aside for them to enter, slamming the door shut behind them, then led them along a passage to a sitting room at the rear of the cottage. Glancing around Arthur noticed that everything was clean, neat and tidy. Looking at the woman he judged her to be about his own age, well-built with a good complexion, and her lightly tanned skin was an indication that she spent a lot of time in the open air. She carried no excess weight, so must work very hard; her eyes were cornflower blue with a twinkle of interest in them. Whilst Olaf was talking to her she pointed to the easy chairs into which they gratefully sank.

Leaving the room for a few moments, she returned with a tray on which was a large jug of milk, three glasses and a plate of flat biscuits. Seating herself, she spoke to Olaf. After quite some time conversing, he turned to Arthur saying, "Well, you are in luck. Jackpot first time. This is Ivor's sister, Stephany. Show her the picture you have."

Arthur took from his pocket the faded photo along with the other papers and handed them to her. She read through the papers, then gazed for some time at the picture she held. Slowly the tears began to flow, and shaken by deep sobs, she tried in vain to stem them. The two men sat in silence, waiting for her grief to abate. Finally sitting up and wiping her eyes dry, she took a deep breath and began talking rapidly to Olaf. She was, Arthur suspected, asking for all the details he had concerning her brother. Several times he asked for confirmation of the meaning of questions put to him. It was nearly an hour later when they paused for breath, and Olaf turned to Arthur to give him a brief outline of the conversation.

"Yes, she is Stephany, and since the death of her mother a few years ago she has lived here alone, often wondering what had happened to her brother. They thought he had escaped from the German army's advance, but were never certain. She had given up all hope of ever knowing the truth, when out of the blue we turn up with the answers. She is overwhelmed that you have gone to all this trouble, and suffered such hardship to find her and bring her this news in order to fulfil your promise to a dying comrade. It will soon be dark. We must return to the village and come back tomorrow for another talk."

Still holding the photo and papers Stephany spoke to Olaf. "She asks if she can keep them for the time being."

"Yes. After all they really are her property."

They turned to leave. She led the way and opened the door, shaking hands with Olaf. She spoke to him for a few moments then, stepping up to Arthur, flung her arms around his shoulders, pulling him towards her and giving him a long lingering kiss on his lips then suddenly releasing him. Arthur staggered backwards blushing like a schoolboy.

"That is her thank you for all you have done," Olaf chuckled. "I am sure that is something you did not expect, but she is so very grateful to you. I think you have gained another conquest here."

Bidding her farewell they walked back into the village, and found the house in which they were billeted. Managing to get a little food, they settled down to sleep intending to return to the cottage tomorrow to complete the story.

The next morning was warm and sunny, but the village seemed almost empty. Only a few men were being handed the meagre rations, and when they lined up for breakfast Olaf asked where everyone was, to be told the army had moved out during the night leaving a rear guard of only a few men. Perhaps this was the push to win control of the pass, they had been involved in earlier.

As soon as they had eaten they set off for the cottage, their papers being checked by the same guard as yesterday. As they reached the gate the door of the cottage was flung open; and Stephany ran to greet them, hugging them each in turn. When they were seated in the sitting room, she produced a tray on which was a large pot of coffee, three mugs and a plate of home-made cakes. Settling down to enjoy this repast, they were soon back to where they had left off the previous night and proceeded to carry on from there, Arthur giving the details, Olaf translating as they went along. She became more animated as the story unfolded and she learnt of the trouble and danger Arthur had had to contend with to reach his destination in order to carry out his promise. She gazed in admiration and spoke rapidly to him. "She is saying," remarked Olaf, "that you are a most exceptional man, being so brave and loyal in your effort to carry out the wishes of her dying brother."

"I must admit," said Arthur, "I did not expect to be involved in another war, or realise hopes of finding any of Ivor's relatives alive after all these years. There is still another document to be given to Stephany." Removing from his pocket a long sealed envelope he said, "This is exactly as it was when Ivor handed it to me with his other papers. According to my friend Father Procovitch the writing on the envelope states 'Only to be opened by my nearest living relative. If none such can be found, then my friend Arthur Hallsworth must take it to his own solicitor to be opened and see that my wishes herein stated are carried out'." With that, he handed her the sealed envelope. With a look of surprise and hands that were trembling she opened it and withdrew from inside a large sheet of paper. Arthur and Olaf watched with interest as she spread it open on the table to read through the contents, noticing her excitement as she came to the end when, with a deep sigh, she handed the letter to Olaf and sat back in her chair. After reading it through he, without a word, handed it back to Arthur who looked surprised as it was written in their language. Taking a closer look he realised there was a translation in English at the bottom of the page. Concentrating on this, he found he was looking at the last will and testament of his deceased friend. This read:

I, Ivor Kaldev, being of sound state of mind, do hereby request that the following instructions be carried out after my death. First, should any of my relatives be found alive when this war ends, then the bequests must go to the nearest one, i.e. mother, sister or brother, or the closest in direct blood line. Should no survivors be found, then my solicitors are instructed to make all bequests herein to my friend Arthur Hallsworth of the town of Kettering in Northamptonshire, or to his next of kin. If, after having made every effort to trace my family and failed, he should also die, I leave all my worldly goods and possessions, according to my above wishes. My solicitors Simpson, Rowlings and Tansley, at 139, Oxford Street, London, WC1, who also hold my official will, are instructed to conduct my business. Signed this 21st day of February 1942 Ivor Kaldev. Witness. James R. Masters Solicitors' clerk, for Simpson, Rowlings and Tansley.

A footnote appended in both languages read:

Whoever presents his/herself to my solicitors to claim this inheritance must be able to prove beyond any reasonable doubt that they are the person they claim to be.

This was signed by the three members of the solicitors acting on Ivor's behalf.

For some moments there was a shocked silence, then all three started talking at once. Holding up his hand, Olaf said, "One at a time, please. Let us hear what Stephany has to say first. After all whatever Ivor has left in his will concerns her the most." The two talked together for some time. He then translated.

"She says she really cannot understand how Ivor could have had anything of value to leave. When he escaped from the Germans, he had very little money and only a few personal possessions. No one knows what happened to him after that, until you met him in the

British army. Stephany is his nearest living relative, and her birth certificate and identification papers prove that. The problem now is how to get her to London to Ivor's solicitors to claim whatever has been left by him. It is going to need a great deal of thought. We had quite enough trouble getting here, and I foresee problems ahead getting back to our depot. How do we achieve getting a permit for her to leave this country and go to England? Perhaps we had better let that be, for the moment."

Stephany rose from her chair and went into the kitchen to prepare a meal. Arthur and Olaf continued to discuss possibilities of getting her to England.

She reappeared carrying a tray with the crockery, cutlery and glasses necessary to lay the table for three. Again going to the kitchen, she returned with large plates of cold meat, cheese and bread and butter, and going over to the beautifully carved sideboard, she removed from a lower cupboard a large bottle, which she showed to Olaf, speaking meanwhile. He turned to explain. "This is their local wine. She wishes us to drink to the memory of Ivor, and to you, for all that you have done to find her and set her mind at rest regarding her brother."

Pouring a glass of wine for each of them, she sat at the table and, raising her glass, gave a toast in her own language. Arthur raised his saying, "Good health, and may everything work out for the best for you, Stephany." When the meal ended, and the table had been cleared, they sat talking for some time, Olaf acting as interpreter. During a lull in the conversation Arthur asked, "What happened to the farm the family once owned?" Olaf questioned Stephany for a while, then explained to him.

"When the German army invaded this part of the country, the farmhouse where she and her mother lived was destroyed; the Germans killed off all the cattle for food, and she and her mother were put into a refugee camp, where her mother eventually died. When the war ended she was released and returned here to find the farm land had been confiscated by the Communists. She has tried to reclaim the value of the farm from her government, but so far has only received a pittance. That is the money she has been living on all these years, supplementing it by selling from the large garden at the rear of this cottage whatever produce she can manage to grow. The previous occupants fled during the war and did not wish to return so, being glad to have found a buyer, sold it to her at a rock bottom price. It is apparent from her lithe figure and the state of her hands that she is a hard working and independent person. She tells me that her produce is sold on the local market every Saturday, so tomorrow she will be gathering the crops in readiness for the next day's market. With what little money she gets from her sales, she buys other foods such as sugar, coffee, flour, meat etc. or barters her goods for dire necessities, and that way she manages to keep her independence. She has no quarrel with the warring factions, and they have not interfered with her way of life, up to date."

Having left the two men together a short while previously, Stephany now appeared clutching a long ageing envelope in her hand, which she held out to Olaf. Opening it he took out some yellowing papers, and after reading them all he held them up in turn. "These are her birth certificate and identity papers, the birth and marriage certificates of her parents, and the birth certificates of Ivor and his brother."

He held up an official looking document with a large seal at the bottom. "This is the title deed to the cottage and land, and here are her release papers from the refugee camp, plus her bank statements for the last two years, all of which should prove without doubt that she is the nearest living relative of Ivor Kaldev."

The sun was beginning to set and clouds were appearing on the horizon. It would soon be dark.

"We must be getting back," Olaf said, "and tomorrow we'll return to help gather the produce, and discuss what possibilities there are of getting her away from here and back to the city. We can then sort things out from there." They got up to leave. She kissed each of them on the cheek, and went to the door to wave farewell to them.

Arriving at the checkpoint, on the return journey to the village, they noticed there was no sentry on duty.

Reaching the house in which they had been billeted it was deserted; there was no sign of the military anywhere, and as they looked round to see if there was any food or drink, to their amazement the door suddenly burst open, and in came an elderly man and woman waving their arms and babbling away. Olaf held up his hand to them, and calming down they spoke to him. Turning to Arthur he translated.

"This is the home of these people which was confiscated by the army. They have been living with their son on the other side of the village, and now that the army has left they have returned to take possession of their home again. We may remain here tonight, and share their supper, but they would like us to leave in the morning."

They joined the old couple for a piece of bread and mug of coffee, then went to the room they had previously used to sleep. Noises down below awakened them at about seven thirty a.m., and they realised the owners were trying to put their home back into some sort of order. Finding there was some water left in the jug on the dressing table they hastily washed, dressed, and went down to the lower floor to be met by the old man, who offered them each a cup of hot coffee for which they were most grateful. Thanking the couple for their hospitality, they picked up their few possessions and left the house.

"What do we do now?" Arthur asked Olaf. He hesitated before replying, "I wonder if Stephany would let us stay at her cottage? We can ask when we get there. If not, we must make other arrangements. We cannot leave here until we know what is happening in the war zone. We have no money, but could offer to pay her when we get out of here. I am sure she would be agreeable to that."

They walked briskly toward the cottage. It was nearing nine a.m. when they arrived and it was apparent that Stephany did not let the grass grow under her feet. She was already busy with a pile of boxes, lining the bottom with newspapers, ready for taking the produce to market the next day. Seeing the two men enter the garden she smiled and hurried towards them holding out her arms to embrace them both. As they entered the house she started talking at length to Olaf, who then translated.

"She says there is a lot of produce to gather and prepare for the market. I have told her we will help, but she insists that we first eat and drink."

As they entered the sitting room, Stephany brought from the kitchen mugs and a jug of milk with plates of cold meat and bread. During the meal Olaf explained their predicament to her, asking if there were a possibility they might stay at her cottage for a short while. She sat back and finished her meal, then looking at them seriously spoke rapidly to Olaf.

"What is her answer?" asked Arthur.

"She is delighted to offer us the use of her home. She feels very lonely at times, and would enjoy our company. We can stay as long as we like. There is no need to bother about paying our way; the help we give in the garden and preparing the produce for market is sufficient for a share of her home and food."

"That is most kind of her," remarked Arthur.

After clearing the breakfast table, Stephany led them upstairs, where they were shown two small rooms each furnished with a single bed, dressing table, wardrobe and the usual hand stand holding wash basin and jug of water. She explained that water for washing could be got from the kitchen tap, and after use the water could be put into the plastic buckets kept for that purpose in the corner of the bedrooms for use in the garden, instead of being wasted.

After unpacking their bits and pieces they went downstairs to be led round to the back of the cottage. The rear garden was very large. Arthur estimated it to be well over an acre of ground and all under cultivation; rows of potatoes, beans, sweet corn, and some vegetables which Arthur did not recognise. Salad crops included lettuce, chives, garlic roots, beetroot and sweet peppers.

"Does she do all this on her own?" he asked Olaf, and after a brief consultation during which she waved her arms over the expanse of the whole garden, he replied:

"Yes. She spends most of her time out here, from early morning until almost dark." Hardly a weed could be seen, Arthur was amazed at her ability to cultivate such a large area alone.

The crops looked healthy and succulent, although the garden tools leaning against the wall of the cottage looked rather primitive compared with the ones he used back home in England, though all were clean and well maintained. She must work very hard he thought, to raise such good quality crops with such outdated implements. She spoke to Olaf and showed him which crops were to be picked for the market. He picked up the large fork, and going to a long row of potatoes he remarked, "I will dig these, and she wants the beans along there gathered. She will show you the ones to pick. Tomorrow we must rise early in order to pick the salad crops, collect the eggs from the bottom of the garden and also cut some heads of cabbage."

They all got down to work and by ten o'clock they had enough produce to fill all the boxes needed for the market next day. The potatoes had to be cleaned and packed, the cabbages checked for pests, and the beans carefully laid down to avoid being damaged. A halt was called then for refreshment – mugs of hot coffee with thick slices of new bread and butter. Resting in the warm sunshine they relaxed for a while, then carried the boxes already packed into the passage of the cottage to be ready for transporting to the market tomorrow.

It was now well past five p.m. and they were all feeling weary. Arthur had to admit that his arms and back were aching. Stephany told them to freshen up whilst she prepared the dinner.

Chapter Twelve

Going up to their respective rooms, they shaved, washed and changed into clean shirts. When they returned to the sitting room the table was already set for the evening meal. Stephany entered from the kitchen carrying a large tureen of meat in gravy, then a dish piled high with vegetables fresh from her own garden. The meal was delicious, and after the table was cleared she brought in the usual large pot of coffee, a bowl of sugar and jug of milk. Arthur was delighted to see milk and sugar – he was not too fond of the strong black coffee which these people seemed to enjoy drinking. Glancing at the clock, Stephany went over to the old fashioned radio and switched on. Music was being played to which they listened for a few minutes, and when it ended an announcer began to speak. Arthur had no idea what was being said, but assumed it to be a news bulletin, as both Olaf and Stephany were giving it their full attention. When the speech ended Stephany turned off the radio and Olaf told Arthur what was happening.

"According to the news, the army contingent who moved out a few days ago from here have now captured the pass, the enemy are in full flight and the retreating forces are being harassed across the plains beyond the mountains. There is a possibility that the leaders of the warring factions may meet, to iron out a peace treaty. This is great news. If they only agree to a ceasefire we may be able to get through to our Red Cross camp on the other side and meet up with one of our convoys. We must listen to the news bulletins each day so that we can assess their progress."

After helping Stephany to clear away the dinner things, they sat down to discuss all possible ways and means of getting back to the city and what chances there were of Stephany going with them. At this she looked doubtful, pointing out to them her concern for the crops and her home. This was a stumbling block they had not anticipated, so an answer had to be found to this problem to enable her to go to

England and claim her inheritance. It was now time to retire so they went to bed leaving many questions unanswered, hoping there would be time to sort them out in the next few days.

Both men slept well, being awakened the next morning by Stephany knocking on the bedroom doors. Their watches showed the time to be nearing six o'clock so they hastily shaved washed and went down to breakfast. In spite of his haste Arthur found that Olaf and Stephany had preceded him, finished their breakfast and were about to clear the table, so making short work of his meal he took his crockery to the kitchen and washed it, and then joined the other two in the garden, helping to cut lettuce and salad vegetables to be packed and loaded with the other produce.

The morning was fresh with the sun just beginning to warm the air. Stephany came from the rear of the cottage with a large heavy handcart onto which the produce was carefully loaded. After locking up the cottage, they set out for the market. Stephany was delighted to have the use of two strong men with the heavy load, making such good time that they were among the first to arrive at the market place, and this meant she could select one of the better vantage points from which to sell her wares. Vendors were setting up their stalls, and the market soon filled up with people ready to make purchases from the variety of goods on offer. By ten o'clock the market was in full swing; horse-drawn carts were arriving, a few oldish cars dropped off customers, and two or three buses had set down passengers. It would seem that now the military had gone people were coming into the town to replenish their supplies. By noon Stephany had sold most of her produce, but Arthur noticed one box full still remaining under the cart. He wondered why these goods had not been offered for sale, when a neatly dressed man approached Stephany. They chatted for a few moments, as did many of her customers. She was evidently a well-known and respected person in the area, but this person seemed to stand apart from the average customer, being better dressed and holding himself with a certain air of confidence.

Having paid over a sum of money for the box of goods, he was about to leave when he turned and spoke to Stephany again. Olaf had been to some of the other traders to obtain some items of which Stephany was in need, and seeing him approaching the gentleman awaited his arrival and spoke to him for quite a while, then turned and offered his hand to Arthur. After a firm hand shake, he smiled at

Stephany and made his way to the stall of another trader. Being more than a little intrigued, Arthur asked, "Who is that? He looks rather an important person."

"Yes," replied Olaf. "He is the mayor of this town and a very influential man hereabouts. He and his wife are very good friends of Stephany, having helped her in many ways on her release from the refugee camp, they gave her several pieces of the furniture she has in the cottage. He was himself a victim of the last war, being held indefinitely in a concentration camp for being a revolutionary. He has no patience with the warring factions causing so much distress in this part of the country. I mentioned a little of our problems to him, and he will be at the cottage this evening to see if there is any way in which he can be of help."

By this time they were all feeling in need of refreshment. It had been a very busy morning and there had been no break since arriving at the market.

"Is there anywhere we might get a bite and drink?" he asked Olaf. He spoke to Stephany who made a reply and pointed to the opposite side of the market.

"We are in luck," he said. "There is a café over there which stays open all day. I think they are called pubs in your country. When the boxes have been packed away, we can all go over and see what they have to offer."

All that was left of the produce was a few bunches of carrots and some greens beginning to wilt; just then a little boy ran up to Stephany with a few coins in his hand. She handed him the leftovers, refusing his money, smiled and ruffled his hair, and the little boy went off, quite pleased with his goods. The empty boxes were collected and tied on to the cart which was then wheeled through the fast emptying market to the café. It was fairly full when they entered and Stephany was offered a seat by a male customer, but when it was realised that the two men were with her, the table was vacated and they all sat down. Arthur and Olaf had no money, as Stephany well knew, so she called the bartender over, spoke to him and he moved away, returning with three large glasses of local beer. They had barely sipped it when a woman came forward and placed before them a large dish of sliced cold meat, with chunks of cheese, followed by a plate of buttered bread slices, plus plates, knives and forks for three.

Stephany handed over the money and they tucked into their meal.

When they had eaten she ordered another glass of beer each. Several customers in the bar came over and spoke to her; there was no doubt of her popularity in the village of Misakev. Finishing the drinks they retrieved the hand cart and set off for the cottage, Stephany and Olaf talking together most of the way home, probably going over the happenings of the day. By the time the cottage was reached the sun was sinking in the west, and Stephany went to the back of the cottage to feed the hens and collect any eggs laid during the day. The two men unloaded the boxes from the cart, and took it round to the back where they helped to water crops that were in need. By this time it was almost dark. They went indoors lit the lamps, and settled down to enjoy a glass of wine with sweet home-made biscuits. It was just after seven p.m. when there was a loud knock on the door which Stephany answered, returning with the gentleman she had conversed with at the market accompanied by an attractive well-dressed middle-aged lady, whom she introduced as the mayor, Mr Jan Patlovic, and his wife Gerda. When they were seated Stephany poured them each a glass of wine, and they then began talking together. Arthur sat in silence being unable to follow the discussion, and although having some idea of what it was about he knew Olaf would explain in due course so he sipped his wine and, being tired, he relaxed.

The four continued talking for well over an hour and Arthur's eyes were beginning to close when he noticed the mayor busily jotting down points on a sheet of paper. It was well past nine before this ended. Olaf looked across at Arthur, saying, "I will try and be brief, so we'll start at the beginning." It was now the turn of the others to sit in silence as he translated.

"In the discussion just held I have explained to the mayor, Jan, what has happened so far regarding the will etc. of Ivor. He is prepared to help as far as is possible. If you will call in his office at the town hall tomorrow morning, he can arrange for you to put a call through from there to Ivor's solicitors in London. You can also contact your bank; there is no bank here, so the transfer of cash will have to be made to the bank in the nearest town from here, which is some forty kilometres away. Jan will be in touch with the manager there, so that as soon as he receives authorisation from England you can draw what money you require. He has also suggested that, now the fighting has ceased in this area, we may be able to get a bus back to our depot. If not, he will endeavour to find some kind of transport to get us there. He realises that Stephany must go to England to claim her inheritance, and has offered to find some one to care for the cottage and garden whilst she is away. He has in view an elderly man who used to be a market gardener. If he will take it on and he and his wife can reside at the cottage then everything should be safeguarded during her absence."

Stephany was quite agreeable to this arrangement, if the elderly couple accepted, which they eventually did, without demur.

"We must then see what transpires after you contact the solicitors tomorrow."

Shortly afterwards the mayor and his wife departed, and they all decided that, after the long tiring day, bed was the best place. Arthur slept well, and woke up to what was going to be a warm sunny day. After a wash and shave, he gave his suit a good brush. Stephany had washed and ironed his shirt so he looked quite neat and tidy for his visit to the town hall. After breakfast he and Olaf set out for the mayor's office, where they were met by his secretary who took them straight to the mayor. Rising from his seat behind the desk he shook hands with them both then motioned for them to sit in the chairs opposite, and the secretary brought in coffee for the three of them. Indicating the telephone, Jan (the mayor) spoke to Olaf, who turned to Arthur with the remark, "It should be a good time to call, as it is about ten thirty a.m. in London; if you have the solicitors' number the phone is all yours."

Arthur took from his pocket the documents giving their office number, checked the directory for the international code for London and carefully dialled the number. It was a few moments before the familiar sound of the British phone system came through, and a few more seconds before he heard a pleasant female voice say, "Simpson, Rowlings and Tansley, Solicitors". Arthur replied immediately:

"This is a long distance call. I wish to speak to the senior partner, Mr Simpson I believe. Would you please put me through to him?"

She replied, "Just a moment sir, I will connect you to his office."

There was a click, and a cultured voice said, "Simpson here. Can I help you?"

Arthur quickly explained.

"I am Arthur Hallsworth and have for some time now been searching for, and have recently found the nearest living relative of one Ivor Kaldev."

"Who? Well I never." A few seconds of silence ensued then, "Please give me the number from which you are calling. I need his file, so I will call back in about ten minutes." Phone number, area code and country were relayed. "Thanks," said Mr Simpson. "I will ring back soon."

The line went dead. Arthur put down the phone and told Olaf what had been said. He translated to the mayor, who spoke a few words into the phone and replaced it. Olaf remarked, "He has told the switchboard to delay all calls for the next half hour, in order to keep the line free for your call from London."

So they relaxed, sat back and drank their coffee. The mayor lit up a rather strong smelling cigarette. They were about to resume their conversation when the phone rang. Arthur lifted it.

"Is that Mr Hallsworth?"

"Yes," he said.

"Mr Simpson here. I have before me the Kaldev file. Who is the relative that you have found?"

"His sister," replied Arthur.

"One moment," came the voice from London. "Ah! Yes, here it is, a sister, Stephany Kaldev; he also mentions his mother Guitter Kaldev."

"She and her son are dead," Arthur told him, "and, as far as we can discover, Stephany is the only living relative."

"I suppose this lady has documents to prove she is who she says she is."

"Oh! yes. She is in possession of all the necessary legal documents; I have had them checked over here, and there is no doubt whatever but that she is the sister of Ivor Kaldev."

A slight pause in London. "Well," said Mr Simpson, "Bring the lady here to our office with her documentary evidence, and we will take things from there. When can you come to England?"

Thinking for a moment or two, Arthur realised it was not going to be that easy to give an exact date.

"Arrangements will be made for us to leave here as soon as possible. We have quite a long journey before we reach an airport from which to get a flight over. I will call you from the place of departure, giving approximate time of arrival. Is it possible for us to be met, and transport provided to get us to your office?"

"Yes, there will be transport to meet you on arrival. In case the office is closed when you arrive, here is my private number. Call me and I will be happy to meet you. If you need any further help, please do not hesitate to contact us. I look forward to meeting you and being able to close this file after all these years. Goodbye Mr Hallsworth, and thank you for all the trouble you have taken in this matter."

Arthur replaced the phone and turning to Olaf explained what had transpired between the solicitor and himself. Olaf translated to Stephany and the mayor. Her eyes sparkling with excitement, she spoke rapidly to them for a few moments, and Olaf remarked, "She is saying how very exciting it all is; she cannot wait to get to your country, never having been out of her own, and to travel has always been one of her dreams."

They sat chatting and drinking coffee for a while, the mayor showing pleasure on Stephany's behalf, saying he hoped it would not be too long before they could leave Misakev.

"We must start planning how to get you to the city."

Arthur was also pleased with the present outcome; he also was getting eager to return home and attend to his own affairs, which had for so long been neglected. They spent quite some time discussing various ways and means of reaching the city, from where they could book their flight to London. Helped by the mayor, transport was arranged as far as the camp being used by convoys of the Red Cross contingent to which Olaf belonged, and from there they hoped to return to the town where Karl and Gerda, the friends of Joseph the lorry driver, lived. They would probably know when Joseph was likely to be calling on his next visit. If they could get a lift back from there with him, it would be a simple matter to get a train to the city, and thence book their flights to London. They returned to the cottage full of anticipation. Stephany was so excited she kept up a stream of questions, some of which Olaf was able to answer. A considerable amount of work still had to be done; things in the garden needed attention, and many other details would have to be completed before they could leave for England.

After supper they all retired, each with their minds occupied with various matters, but sleep eventually overtook them. It was a bright sunny morning when the three of them arose to start a new day taking breakfast together. Stephany still had an air of suppressed excitement about her, and Arthur noticed that her slightly flushed face gave her quite a pretty look. Whenever their glances met she smiled, seeming to thank him for everything. Arthur also had to admit to a feeling of self satisfaction at having got this far in his quest to find Ivor's next of kin.

A busy day was spent in the garden, and just as they were about to start the evening meal the elderly man recommended to Stephany by the mayor had been contacted by him and had arrived to discuss the details of what would be expected of he and his wife. He was weather-beaten, with greying hair, which made him look much older than his fifty-two years. They talked together for some considerable time, and he seemed interested and agreeable to what was required. He rose from his chair, shook hands with each of them, and left. Olaf then explained the outcome of the conversation to Arthur.

"He is bringing his wife over tomorrow. If she is agreeable, then they will accept the job. He has named his price for tending the garden, and selling the produce in the market each week. They will live in the cottage, until Stephany's return, thus being on the spot to attend to the many and varied chores."

This arrangement was satisfactory to Stephany, who seemed quite happy to leave her home and garden to the care of the elderly couple during her absence. After the meal, the men went outside to sit in the cool evening air with a glass of wine; Stephany excused herself, and went up to her room, from whence they soon heard her singing one of the local folk songs. When she later came down her explanation was that she had been sorting out her clothes for the coming journey. They laughed at her, and she blushed.

Going inside they had another short discussion in an endeavour to iron out some of the last few problems, then retired. The next day a start was made on the garden produce that had to be got ready for the market. Whilst they were all busy, the elderly man and his wife arrived; she was a portly, kindly-looking woman, seemingly some years younger than her husband. Stephany took her on a tour of the cottage, whilst he undertook a study of the garden, being much impressed with the quality of the produce and having no doubt as to his ability to cope with it and the sales. They later sat down together for a coffee, and finalised the agreed terms. The man was to keep careful records of all sales, putting the proceeds into Stephany's bank account, less any expenses which might arise. They shook hands on the deal on the understanding that the mayor would inform them of

Stephany's departure and hand the key over for them to take up residence. The couple left and the three toasted their success to date with a glass of local wine.

The next day when they arrived at the market to sell the produce, the mayor was there to greet them with the news of there being a possibility of available transport to get them back to the camp site, leaving tomorrow (Sunday) morning. They must be at the town hall before the departure time of eleven a.m. He also offered to inform the elderly couple they could take over the cottage on Monday morning.

The mayor then handed Arthur a large envelope, containing authorisation from his bank for £1,000 to be put at his disposal from his account. Leaving the other two to attend the stall, he hurried over to the bank to withdraw £300, leaving the rest to be drawn from the city bank to meet the cost of their air fares to London. The day went well; news of her impending departure must have reached Stephany's friends, as many of them came over to shake hands with her and wish her good luck. By late afternoon all but a few wilting items of the produce had been sold, and when the same cheerful little boy turned up and offered a few coins for the leftovers, as usual Stephany handed them to him without accepting his money. Olaf explained, "His mother is a very poor widow with several children, so the stallholders who can give a little something to help, at the end of market days."

They quickly cleared up, stacking and tying the boxes on to the cart. They crossed to the other side of the market place, and entered the café. Going into the respective public conveniences, each had a wash and brush up, and feeling fresh and clean they sat at an empty table and ordered a meal, with a large glass of beer each. The proprietor served the meal, telling them it was on the house; he wished them good luck, *Bon Voyage*, and a safe return when their business was completed.

Chapter Thirteen

The café soon became crowded, mainly with market traders all chatting more cheerfully than of late. It would appear from the conversation that the main topic concerned the talks still taking place at the peace conference table, as boundaries and other small matters had yet to be agreed. Everyone hoped that this would be the end of hostilities, and peace for both ethnic tribes from now on. This was good news for Arthur and his friends as it meant a much safer journey for them.

Returning to the cottage they all proceeded to pack. It did not take Arthur and Olaf long as they had few possessions, and Arthur's effects were at the Red Cross station, being cared for by his friends. Like most ladies, Stephany was agonising over the suitability of which dresses and things to take. Arthur asked Olaf to explain to her that she must not pack too much; they had to travel as light as possible, and some time later she brought down a rather shabby suitcase and a holdall. Smiling, she placed them in the passage ready for morning. She then went and prepared the supper, after which they sat talking for a while, pleased and excited that, after all the previous problems they had encountered, all was now going along so well. Having decided that all had been done that could be done, they retired.

Awaking the next morning to grey skies and a slight drizzle, they ate a hasty breakfast, and looked round to ensure that all was well. As they were about to leave, the elderly man came through the garden gate, and spoke to Stephany. After listening to her for a few moments, he seemed satisfied with what she had told him. Locking the cottage door, she handed him the key; the three then picked up their luggage and set off for the town hall. With tears in her eyes Stephany looked back at the cottage. She hesitated for a moment then, bracing her shoulders turned and walked on with her friends. Arthur understood how she must feel. This had been her home for many years, holding memories for her. She had never been out of the area since birth, with the exception of her stay in the refugee camp and that was only a few miles distant. This must be a great new experience for her. He could see the excitement showing on her face, making her look much younger than her fifty-six years. He noticed how upright and healthy-looking her slim, well-formed body was, being slightly tanned from her out of doors activities in the garden; her blonde hair neatly combed and brushed bounced as she strode along, her cornflower blue eyes were sparkling in anticipation of the adventure ahead. She carried on an animated conversation with Olaf, and falling into step beside them Arthur wondered why it was that he had not noticed Stephany's charm before. When they arrived at the town hall the mayor and his wife were waiting for them, and after shaking hands the mayor handed Arthur a bag containing food to refresh them on their journey. They thanked him and stood talking together.

The rain had ceased, and a promise of sunshine emerged through the clouds which was just as well, for when the transport arrived it turned out to be a rather ancient farm vehicle open at the back, with a number of sacks and bales of some sort apparently meant to be used as seating. The driver, a young-looking man of about twenty-five, got down from the cab and spoke to the mayor who introduced him to his three passengers with whom he shook hands, then turning to Arthur exclaimed, "Ah! you are English. Good. I also speak a little English, so we can talk, I learn at high school for two years but can never use it until now."

He offered Stephany the seat beside himself at the front; Arthur and Olaf climbed into the back and made themselves comfortable on the bales, which were surprisingly nice and soft. The clouds had dispersed and the sun shone brightly. The mayor and his wife wished them a safe and pleasant journey, assuring them the war was at an end; an armistice had been signed and there would be no trouble on their way through the pass; they expressed fond hopes that the travellers would return when everything had been settled in England.

Arthur promised to do so, again thanking him for all his help. Then, with a grating of gears, the driver moved off and they waved back as they turned the corner. The town soon disappeared into the distance and they were fast approaching the hills, where they had seen so much of war and death.

Reaching the pass through the mountains, the driver pulled to a stop beneath the shade of a large roadside tree and suggested they now have a meal. Bringing out a large box containing sandwiches of thick bread and meat, he handed them round. Arthur then produced from the bag the mayor had given him some home-made cakes, and two large bottles of the local wine and there, seated on the grass, cool in the shade, they all enjoyed the simple meal. The driver sat beside Arthur, seemingly eager to make conversation. He was a small farmer, released from the army after the recent signing of the armistice and had just returned home to his family. His wife had managed to keep things going during his absence, and this was the first load he was taking to town since his return.

"What is in the bales?" asked Arthur.

"Wool," he replied. "A very special kind mixed from sheep's wool and angora which is fetching a good price on the market just now, money which we are badly in need of for buying seeds for next year's crops. The ten bales I have here will provide for that, and leave sufficient to purchase food for the family. How glad I am that the war is over. Had it gone on much longer we would have lost our home and land."

Arthur then told him a little of his own experiences in the last war, which meant they had something in common. When the meal was finished, Stephany decided to change places with Arthur. She found the cab noisy and uncomfortable, preferring to travel in the fresh air and sunshine. The driver and Arthur were thus able to carry on with their talk, whilst Olaf pointed out the area where the battle had been fought at which he and Arthur had been taken prisoners. Stephany looked very upset seeing the war-torn area, and thinking of all the young men who had been killed and wounded for nothing.

By four o'clock they were at the camp site of the Red Cross convoy, which appeared to have been deserted for some time. They took this opportunity of making a call of nature, Stephany being able to find a suitable rock behind which to hide; they then drove on. The sun was beginning to set when they came to a signpost indicating seventy kilometres to the town where Arthur's friend lived. There was very little traffic on the road, so they were able to make good progress and soon arrived at the Red Cross station. Some of Olaf's team were still there, delighted to see their officer back safe and well. They gathered round, all talking at once, and quite surprised to see Stephany with them. Hastily explaining who she was, he asked one of his men to take a car and transport her and Arthur to the local hotel for the night. Arthur collected the possessions left behind on that fateful day which now seemed so long ago. As they both got into the car, he recognised the driver as one of the men who had accompanied the convoy on that day. Arriving at the modest hotel, they were fortunate to find two single rooms available.

The receptionist spoke a little English and explained that it was too late for a meal to be served, but she would arrange for sandwiches and coffee to be sent to their rooms in about half an hour. Arthur took the luggage upstairs to their rooms, and unlocking a door he handed the key to Stephany who, looking a little wary and surprised at everything, entered. Placing her cases by the bed he pointed to the wardrobe. She sat on the bed, jigged up and down for a moment, smiled at Arthur then lay back and gave a deep sigh. He smiled back, went into the corridor and crossed to his own room. They were quite comfortably furnished and he was pleased to see that the bathroom adjoined his room. 'A bath,' he thought. 'That is something I really need but I must first offer it to Stephany.' He returned to her room to find her still laying on the bed, gazing at the ceiling. Taking her by the hand he gently led her to the bathroom. She peeped in and looked delighted. Making her understand she could use it first, she dashed to her room for toiletries and towel. He soon heard the bath water running.

Whilst he was unpacking a few of his essentials, a maid arrived carrying a tray on which was a plate of freshly made ham sandwiches and a large pot of hot coffee, sugar and milk which she placed on the bedside table, and departed. He heard Stephany go to her room so made for the bathroom; hot water to shave with, plus the added luxury of a lovely hot bath.

He was tempted to linger, but the pangs of hunger overcame the desire, so he towelled briskly and put on a clean shirt and trousers and returned to his room to find Stephany sitting on his bed, attired in some sort of old fashioned housecoat, eating a sandwich with a cup of coffee close by. Looking up at him she smiled, meanwhile adjusting her housecoat to cover her breasts. Handing him the plate of sandwiches, she poured him a cup of coffee, then sat in silence looking demure, her smile widening a little. They knew little of each other's language, but managed to make conversation at a level of understanding. Both felt clean and relaxed after the tiring journey, and for Arthur at least it was good to be back in civilisation once more. He ate and enjoyed his sandwiches; the coffee was hot and as milk and sugar had been provided it was just to his liking. Noticing his cup was empty Stephany picked up the pot and leaned forward to refill it, but this time, when the front of her coat fell open, she made no attempt to close it. Arthur could not help noticing how firm her breasts were and thought, for someone her age, she must have looked after herself well. Feeling embarrassed he looked away, hoping she had not noticed his interest, but he blushed as he felt a thrill of excitement running through him. Having finished their refreshment Stephany rose. Looking down at Arthur for a moment, she then bent and kissed him gently on the lips. The kiss was soft but firm, with surely a hidden meaning in it. Arthur felt his blood pressure rising, it had been a long time since a kiss had managed to arouse in him feelings of sexual desire. I must stop these kinds of thoughts he mused. She is only showing her thanks for everything.

Stephany left his room and he heard her door close. He undressed, put on his pyjamas and climbed into bed, lying awake for some time with thoughts of what might be ahead for her. Then, plumping up his pillow, he put out the light and drifted off to sleep. He awoke at about three o'clock the next morning and, from the dim light filtering through the curtains at the window, saw there was someone in his room. His first thought was a burglar, and keeping perfectly still he lay ready to grab the person who was slowly moving toward the bed. When near enough Arthur's hand shot out and grabbed the wrist of the intruder who gave a sharp cry of pain. Still holding on, Arthur leaned over and switched on his bedside lamp. To his amazement he found himself holding on to Stephany. She wriggled to free herself from his painful hold. He released her and sat speechless for a moment; she sat rubbing her wrist. By this time Arthur had regained his composure and, looking at her, realised she was clad only in a very thin nightgown; her cheeks were flushed and her bosom rising and falling from her recent exertions. Arthur apologised saying:

"I did not realise it was you. Why have you come into my bedroom?"

Stephany looked puzzled for a moment, then must have understood as she murmured in English:

"Not sleep."

He guessed that, being in a strange place, she was finding it difficult to sleep, and before he could answer, she spoke again.

"Me stay with you please."

'Oh dear,' thought Arthur. 'Now what do I do?' She looked tired and nervous and needed comforting so he threw back the covers and she slid into his bed. He did the same and turned off the light. They lay side by side for a while, not moving, then he felt her gently edging nearer to him. He lay on his side, his back towards her, trying to fight off the urge of desire awakening within him. Her arms encircled him, and as she came closer he could feel the warmth of her body and the firm breasts pressing into his back. Stephany let out a long sigh. Was it relief or sexual pleasure, thought Arthur, trying to keep his feelings in check. Her hand was resting on his bare chest inside his pyjama jacket. He half turned towards her to be met with a lingering kiss as she drew him closer. He was fast becoming aroused and it seemed that she was too. This is not the time or place for this he thought. I must cool things down before we do something we may later regret. He lay still; Stephany, holding him close, moved slightly to make herself more comfortable. It was as much as Arthur could do not to put his arms around her and return the kiss, but he resisted the temptation. Her soft regular breathing soon made him realise that she was fast asleep, and pulling the covers up over her shoulders he eased her arm from around him. Making himself comfortable he tried to get some sleep but was conscious all the time of her warm body lying beside him, plus the smell of sensuous womanly perfume such as he had not experienced for some years left him feeling confused, but eventually sleep took over.

He awoke to find the early morning sun shining through the window. Not sure at first where he was, he sat up and then saw Stephany lying beside him, the bed covers had slipped off her and her thin gown had become ruffled up to her thighs. Her long tanned legs exposed, she lay slightly on her right side breathing steadily, and with one breast peeping from the top of her nightgown she looked even younger asleep. Arthur could not but admire her; she was a most desirable female, but was she right for him? He then thought of the implication if someone came into the room and found them together. He went to her room collected her clothes and placed them on his bed. Gathering up his own clothes he decided to take over the bathroom; having shaved, washed and dressed he then looked in to see if Stephany was awake. She was sitting up in bed rubbing her eyes, and gazed at Arthur in surprise until she realised where she was. Climbing out of bed she smiled and said, "Good morning", then picked up her clothes to go to the bathroom. When she later emerged she was dressed and ready for breakfast, seemingly quite unconcerned that she had slept in his bed with him.

After breakfast they went to their rooms and packed. When settling the account Arthur asked if there was a taxi available to take them to the address of his friends. When they arrived Gerda was overjoyed to see them, but a little puzzled at first as to where Stephany fitted in. When Karl arrived home, all was soon explained. Karl also told them that Joseph was to be expected tomorrow or the next day, so they were offered bed and meals. The four of them went out for the evening, looking around and having a drink in a favourite bar of Karl and Gerda. Everything was new to Stephany. She enjoyed this unusual outing, becoming quite excited at the sight of the large shops filled with all manner of luxury goods such as she had never before seen, lingering longest at the ladies' fashion stores. They came home rather late and as there was only one spare room it was given to Stephany, whilst Arthur was made comfortable on the couch in the lounge. At least, he thought, I shall not be tempted by Stephany tonight, she seems to be getting closer to me each day, holding my hand at every opportunity, and her kisses are no longer just a friendly greeting, I feel quite a lot of passion from them. He knew she had never been married, but had she ever been made love to by a man? There must have been men in her life in the past. She was no amateur at kissing. He wondered whether to let things go on, or nip them in the bud now.

He realised how deep for her his feelings were becoming. She was a very desirable woman, and things could turn out to be romantic after all. As a widower he was a fair catch. He knew of a few widows back home who would be only too willing to share life with him, but still retaining loving memories of his late wife, he had so far resisted getting involved. He fell asleep to be awakened by Gerda clad in her housecoat bringing in the breakfast. Hastily leaving the room and finding the bathroom empty he quickly shaved, washed, dressed and went down to breakfast. Stephany soon appeared, and Gerda came down already dressed for going out. The two sat chatting throughout the meal. When Arthur asked of Karl, he was handed a note. Written by him before leaving for work it read:

Joseph expected in time for evening meal. Make yourself at home. I understand the ladies are going out shopping. If you wish to stay at home there are some English books on the shelves. Help yourself, see you about six this evening.

The women cleared away and washed up the breakfast things then, picking up a large shopping bag each, looked at Arthur expectantly, implying, "Did he wish to accompany them?" When he shook his head, Gerda wrote the name of a restaurant on a piece of paper with one o'clock added. Handing it to him she made a motion of eating, pointing to all three of them. Arthur nodded that he understood they wished him to meet them there for a meal at that time; they then left.

Stephany's eyes were sparkling, her cheeks glowing with excitement. This was the first time in her life she had been shopping in a large store, and had been able to obtain up to date fashions for ladies. To his surprise Arthur found on the bookshelf one of the Hammond Innes novels which he had not yet read, so he took it and settled down in the back garden to read and relax. It was a pleasant morning and he was glad to shed some of his responsibilities for a while. He must have dozed off to sleep for he was dreaming of Stephany and awoke with a start. Peering at his watch he found to his dismay it was nearing noon. He went indoors, freshened up and put on a tie, then locked up the house and set off at a steady pace. He had an idea where the restaurant was situated, having passed it the previous evening, but it was quite a journey and he did not want to be late. Arriving at about twelve forty, he looked around but there was no sign of the two ladies, so he went to the bar and ordered a beer. The place was rapidly filling up, so he went to find the head waiter, who fortunately spoke a little English and booked a table for three for one o'clock.

Keeping an eye on the door whilst sipping his drink, he awaited their arrival. It was a few minutes after one p.m. when they entered the restaurant and, looking round, saw Arthur at the bar. They rushed over, the shopping bags now heavy with purchases, and both talked at once. Arthur gave them each a kiss on the cheek, not daring to let Stephany find his lips. Seeing the party was now complete the head waiter led them to a table where, with his help, they ordered their meal and a bottle of wine. Arthur settled down to enjoy the food, leaving the ladies to continue talking. He could see that Stephany was bubbling over with excitement and, by the amount of parcels in their bags, they had certainly enjoyed the shopping spree. He hoped Stephany had not spent all her ready cash, but he knew all that she required could be had from the bank when they reached the city. He was pleased to see how well the two girls were getting on together, cementing what was likely to be a firm friendship. The meal over, Arthur paid the bill and picked up some of the heavier parcels to carry.

Strolling steadily along it was nearing four p.m. when they arrived home. The girls sorted out the purchases then disappeared upstairs, where for quite some time, much to his amusement, he heard them giggling and chattering like a couple of schoolgirls. Gerda then entered the room and, going behind him, she placed her hands over his eyes saying what he took to be "You must not look". Stephany then entered the room and Gerda took her hands away. He blinked for a moment then saw Stephany standing before him all smiles. He could not believe his eyes. With the exception of her blonde hair and cornflower blue eyes she was completely transformed from a middle-aged woman to a smartly dressed younger looking one wearing nylons for the first time, a new dress, shoes and make-up. She looked ten or twelve years younger. She spun round to show off her dress, which lifted to allow her legs above the knee to be viewed. Arthur stood spellbound, his heart beating a rapid tattoo as he thought, by God, she really is lovely. Stephany watched, waiting for his approval, which was given without hesitation. He rose and held out his arms to her, and she rushed forward, offering her lips. They kissed in front of Gerda without embarrassment. She laughed happily and Stephany blushed. She had been in love with him from the day he and Olaf had found her at her cottage, and now she felt he was falling in love with her.

Gerda unpacked her own new dress and showed it to Arthur, then went to prepare the evening meal. Karl arrived home soon after six o'clock and was most impressed by the change in Stephany. He was shown, and approved, his wife's selection, but could not take his eyes off Stephany. Joseph came in just as the meal was being served and was introduced to Stephany. Karl spoke to Joseph and laughed, then turning to Arthur Joseph remarked:

"I interpret for Karl. He say you are a sly old dog, you have found yourself a lovely woman who changes from peasant girl to princess all in one day."

After the meal they sat together sharing a bottle of wine, whilst Arthur related many of the incidents experienced in the weeks since his departure. Arrangements were then made for the following day. Joseph had finished his deliveries and was returning to his depot in the market town near the village of Mirmskov from where all this had started. Being due back there by midday, it would necessitate an early start so they all retired. Arthur and Joseph shared the lounge, Arthur sleeping on the settee, Joseph curled up on the two armchairs placed together. They were awakened at six a.m., and after using the bathroom they all had breakfast. Luggage was then collected and Gerda handed Joseph a packet of food and a bottle of wine for the journey. Karl shook hands all round, but there were tears in Gerda's eyes as she kissed Stephany and Arthur farewell, and they set off for the depot where Joseph had parked his lorry. After checking that everything was in good order, and that there was plenty of room in the cab for the three of them, they climbed aboard. Arthur noticed that Stephany had sensibly put on her old clothes in which to travel, but she still looked radiant. They made good time and stopped just before noon for the meal during which time Arthur explained to Joseph all that had happened to him since he had previously left his friends, Karl and Gerda.

Chapter Fourteen

Joseph was intrigued to hear of their adventures, and stated that the war was now well and truly over, the two parties having agreed to terms and the area of the country in which he lived was now at peace. He was most interested to learn that Stephany was on her way with Arthur to London in order to claim her inheritance, and hoped all would turn out well for her. They chatted away for some time in their own language, then she slowly nodded off to sleep. Joseph then turned to Arthur saying:

"I hope you are aware that this lady is head over heels in love with you. She has been singing your praises for some time; according to her you are the most wonderful man she has ever met and hopes that one day you will love her. She realises there are differences in country backgrounds, religions, etc. but I think she would be happy to settle down anywhere, so long as you were there."

Arthur remained silent for a while then, letting out a deep sigh replied to Joseph's comments:

"Yes, I do see she has fallen in love and must admit to similar feelings for her. She is an exceptional woman and I am sure would make an admirable wife, but there are many difficulties to be overcome – not only in England but in her own country. This is the first time she has travelled and she may not be able to adjust; our ways are totally different and things move at a much faster pace in England. Homesickness could overtake her, making her wish to return to the only way of life to which she has been accustomed. However we can jump the hurdles as we reach them, after seeing the solicitors dealing with Ivor's will and when she has met my family."

"I think you underestimate her," Joseph replied. "If you are there I feel certain you will find she will adjust."

They sat in silence as Stephany stirred then, fully awake, looked them both over before resuming her chat with Joseph, no doubt telling him of her future plans, thought Arthur as, putting her arm through his, she snuggled up to him smiling and looking quite happy and contented. They arrived at the depot mid-afternoon and Joseph enquired where they would be staying prior to arrangements being made for them to get to the city and airport.

"I think probably a hotel," replied Arthur.

"What about your friends at the bar? I'm sure they would love to have you both. Wait, I will ring from here."

He went into the office, returning a few minutes later all smiles and saying, "You are very welcome to stay with them. They would have been most disappointed had you gone to a hotel, and they are waiting to see you, anxious to hear of your adventures. Put your luggage into the boot of my car, and I will run you round there."

They were soon outside the bar where the door was immediately thrown open and they were greeted like long lost friends. A meal was on the table including a large glass of best beer for each of them, after which they sat around in the parlour listening to what had happened to Arthur since he left, Gregor translating for his wife.

They soon made friends with Stephany whom they admired, and when it was time for the bar to open, Lenie took her upstairs to have a bath and change of clothes and when she came down she was wearing a new outfit, looking so young and happy that Arthur's heart beat a little faster as he joined her and they went into the bar together, which soon began to fill. There were many admiring glances cast at Stephany by men drinking at the bar, but when a tall good looking man of about thirty or so came over and engaged Stephany in conversation, Arthur felt a stab of jealousy. He had no idea of what was being said but noticed a slight blush appearing on her cheeks, making her look even more attractive, as her eyes sparkled from the attention she was getting. Lenie came from behind the bar and sat with them. She spoke to the young man who, with a look of keen interest on his face, made his way back to the bar. They spent a happy time talking and drinking a beer or two until the bar closed, then going into the parlour to discuss plans for them getting to the city and the airport. Goodnights were said and, at the top of the stairs, Stephany held on to Arthur tightly for a moment giving him a passionate kiss. She released him and walked into her own room; he was relieved to find there was a long passage between their rooms and hoped she would not repeat the intrusion into his bed fearing that he would be unable to control his feelings for her if she did so.

However, both were tired from the journey and excitement, and were soon fast asleep.

The next morning they went to the bank, and meeting with no problems there, each withdrew a required amount of money then walked to the travel agents to enquire the best way to the city. The agent was most helpful; consulting a train timetable, he arranged for the tickets and also rang the airport, being pleased to tell them there were seats available on a flight to Heathrow the following Wednesday leaving at five p.m. "Should he book two?" Arthur nodded, making a note of the flight no. "Your tickets will be here on Monday morning."

With that problem settled, they then took a walk round the market where at one of the stalls they met Lenie. The two women conversed for some time, then taking Stephany's arm Lenie led her away towards the shops on the other side of the market, and when Arthur began to follow she shook her head and, pointing to the café opposite, gave him to understand they would eat there at twelve thirty, so Arthur was left to wander around the market alone. He found it quite interesting and time passed so quickly he was surprised when he walked over to the café to find the two women already there seated at a table, Stephany holding several parcels and looking slightly embarrassed. Lenie ordered sandwiches and coffee which they enjoyed, plus a much needed rest, returning to the bar just as Gregor was about to close. Stephany went straight up to her room, reappearing in time for the evening meal.

The evening was again spent in the bar, Stephany making friends with many of the customers who joined them at their table, being keenly interested in Arthur's adventures. As Sunday was a quiet day, Gregor proposed an early lunch, and when the bar was closed, for all to go to Mirmskov to call on the widow Jaunta and Father Procovitch, the priest, in order to let them know of the success of the quest. On the way to the village it was decided to call on the priest first and take him to the widow's cottage so they could all be together to hear of the events which had happened since Arthur's departure all those weeks ago. The priest was overjoyed at his return and, when introduced to Stephany once more attired in her new finery, showed his admiration of her. During the journey to the cottage he turned to Arthur, saying:

"The widow was hoping to see you again before you left for England as she has a pleasant surprise awaiting you."

Seeing the car pull up at the gate, the widow ran out to greet them. Shaking hands with the priest, she embraced Arthur and was introduced to Stephany. Leading them into the cottage, she produced mugs of coffee all round and they sat down to hear all about Arthur's quest. Everyone sat entranced as the story unfolded, with Gregor translating. Just as the story neared its end there was a knock on the door which the widow answered, returning with a well set up man of some sixty years or so, and although weather beaten with hair greying at the temples, his twinkling blue eyes and cheerful smile gave him a friendly appearance. The priest rose from his chair to make the necessary introductions in his own language. Arthur sat wondering what all this was about, when the priest turned to him, saying:

"This is the widow's surprise. Allow me to introduce Mr Peter Dumrov, a widower and childhood friend of the widow Jaunta. He owns a large farm nearby, and having recently met again and getting on very well together, they hope shortly to marry. I have given them my blessing."

Arthur was delighted that the widow had found someone with whom to share her life; they seemed well suited to each other, and he was also relieved that she had overcome her infatuation for him.

With preparations for the evening service to be made, the priest regretfully had to say farewell. Gregor also realised that time was fleeting and the bar would soon have to be opened, so with many hugs and kisses they went their separate ways, arriving in good time to open for the evening trade. Once again the evening was spent in convivial company in the bar. The next day Arthur and Stephany called in at the bank to replenish their dwindling cash resources, then going on to the travel agents to collect their tickets for the flight to Heathrow. Arthur wondered how Stephany was placed financially, as she seemed to have spent money freely when shopping with Lenie the other day; she still had not divulged what she had bought.

Her withdrawal today had been quite substantial so he assumed there was no cause for alarm. The rest of the day was spent exploring the city, and the following day both were busy packing in readiness for leaving early on Wednesday morning to get to the airport. Gregor had organised a farewell party that evening for them which proved to be most enjoyable; a very happy occasion. When the bar was closed and cleaned they all retired, knowing an early start had to be made in the morning.

Both ate a good breakfast, and Gregor drove them to the station in time to catch the train. He wished them good luck, a safe and pleasant journey, with the hope that they would one day return to see them all again. The journey passed without incident, Arthur dozing at intervals, but Stephany remaining awake throughout watching with interest the lovely scenery. Arriving in the city, Arthur took a taxi to the airport where they were well ahead of the time required for booking in, so went to the snackbar for refreshments. Stephany could not take her eyes off the planes standing on the tarmac outside. Arthur began to wonder what her reaction would be on her first flight; would she be afraid or even air sick? Having passed through security check, they came to passport control – Stephany's passport so shiny new beside Arthur's battered old one.

The flight was called and having requested seats in the non-smoking area the stewardess showed them to their seats. When settled Arthur fixed her seat belt. She looked anxious and gave him a wan smile, and smiling back he took her hand in his, trying to instil some confidence in her. The jets began to increase in velocity and suddenly the plane was racing down the runway and with just a gentle bump rose up into the clear blue sky. Stephany gripped his hand tighter, then as the plane levelled out seemed to relax but she still looked pale. About an hour later the stewardess served a light meal with a choice of drinks, coffee, wine or beer. Being thirsty Arthur settled for a beer, whilst Stephany chose coffee. Both were hungry so it did not take long to eat the meal supplied. Each then took another cup of coffee, when Stephany, her head resting on Arthur's shoulder holding firmly on to his hand, was soon dozing. Some considerable time elapsed, when over the tannoy came the announcement, "Please fasten your safety belts, we are approaching Heathrow and should be landing in about twenty minutes. The weather in London is warm and dry, the temperature is 21°C. Please check that you have all your hand luggage before leaving the plane; we hope you have enjoyed a pleasant flight."

Stephany awoke as Arthur leaned over to fit her belt into place. He pointed down through the window beside her, and there below stretching out for miles lay the green and pleasant English countryside.

Stephany watched spellbound. Before long the scenery changed. They were now flying over London, and she was amazed at its vastness. The plane circled then began to descend and with only a slight bump or two touched down on the runway where it taxied to the airport Buildings and came to a stop. Arthur's "Welcome to England" remark was met with a smiling "Thank you". Collecting the hand luggage they left the plane, going through passport control and into the heavy luggage claim area. Stephany watched with interest as case after case came round on the carousel, and seeing their cases come round Arthur grabbed them, loaded them onto a luggage trolley and went through customs inspection without problems; then they found themselves out on the Heathrow concourse. Stephany was taken by surprise at seeing hundreds of people milling around.

Entering an empty phone booth Arthur found the solicitors' number and rang them. For some moments there was no answer then a female voice said, "Simpson, Rowlings and Tansley Solicitors."

"This is Mr Arthur Hallsworth. I was told to ring you on arrival at Heathrow."

"Just a moment," came the reply. "The office is closed, but Mr Simpson left a message that, should you ring, I was to contact him, and his car and chauffeur would be put at your disposal to get you to your home. Would you leave your home phone number please, and Mr Simpson will ring tomorrow and make an appointment for you to come to the office."

Arthur gave his home number and the voice then said, "Thank you, a car will be at Heathrow within half an hour. Please wait near the information desk, where the driver will look for you."

With the arrangements completed they found a seat near the desk, sat down and waited. Stephany, watching all that was going on around her, seemed mesmerised. He could see she was bursting to ask questions, but her limited knowledge of the English language prevented her doing so. She could only gaze around and wonder at the hustle and bustle going on at this, the busiest airport in the world. A chauffeur appeared at the desk holding up a hastily written card bearing the name Mr Hallsworth. Arthur signalled to him, and he came over saying, "I have orders to take you to your home," and picking up their luggage led them out to the car. Arthur was most impressed with the Bentley standing at the kerb. When all were seated, the driver turned to say, "I understand you live in Kettering, so I will take the M6 and branch over to the M1. With luck we should reach your home before midnight." Weaving its way out of

Heathrow the car was soon speeding along the motorway, meeting with little traffic on the way. They had a good clear run into the Midlands, and being dark by this time Stephany was unable to enjoy the scenery, so lay her head on Arthur's shoulder and dropped off to sleep.

It took a little over an hour and a quarter to reach the outskirts of the town, and when the driver slowed down and turned to Arthur saying, "You will have to direct me from here," Arthur leaned forward pointing the way and within minutes they pulled up before his home. All was in darkness. Going to the front door he unlocked it and entered, switching on the light in the hall; meanwhile the driver had unloaded their luggage and handed it to him. He thanked him and gave him a very generous tip, then went to Stephany who stood in the drive gazing up at the house. Placing an arm round her waist he led her inside. As the door closed she threw her arms around him kissing him with passionate abandon. He led her to the kitchen, and opening the fridge door he found to his surprise that it was well stocked; their return had evidently been expected so, like all English people on the return home, his first thought was for a cup of tea. He put on the kettle, whilst Stephany took to exploring his home, moving from room to room admiring everything she saw. He brewed his tea but made her a cup of coffee and they sat in the kitchen relaxing, each tentatively wondering what tomorrow might have in store for them both. Now the strain of the long journey was beginning to be felt, so they ate a few sandwiches.

Then Arthur carried the luggage up to their bedrooms, and placing Stephany's case on the bed in a spare room he kissed her then led her to the bathroom where he left her, and went into his own room. Stephany followed him and, taking his arm, persuaded him to return to the bathroom with her where she pointed to the shower. Realising she did not know what it was, he adjusted it, demonstrated how to use it and turned it on. She gave him a delightful smile, and started to undress. Feeling a little embarrassed he returned to his room and proceeded to unpack his case, and as he was hanging up the last of his clothes, Stephany entered the room clad only in the most daring oyster coloured negligee which, although covering her body, hid nothing of her charms. Arthur could not take his eyes off her. She went over and sat on his bed, saying something he did not understand, but her intentions were quite apparent for she made no attempt to return to her own room. Arthur went to the bathroom from where he heard her unpacking in her own room. After a shower he completed his toilet, put on pyjamas, went to his own room, and was just about to get into bed when Stephany stepped in and closed the door, still attired in her flimsy gown. He gazed in shocked surprise as she slipped it off and stood naked before him, and as her breathing increased the look of passionate desire in her eyes made her cheeks glow. With breasts firmly protruding she slipped easily between the sheets, pulling Arthur down beside her.

Stroking his hair and pressing her body close to him, his heart missed a beat, then began to thump. She was a most desirable woman. Arthur struggled with his conscience for a few moments, then his reserve gave way. They embraced in passionate kissing and exploration of each other's bodies, then slowly and gently he penetrated her. Within moments they were united in their desire for each other which ended with her cry of ecstasy and his sigh of contentment. They kissed and she held him tightly, then both dropped off into a deep relaxing sleep.

They awoke to the sound of a downpour of rain; Stephany got out of bed and made for the bathroom. Arthur lay for some time thinking of all that had happened in the night. He had no doubt but that she loved him, and he now felt sure of his feelings for her but what was likely to happen at their meeting with the solicitor? Donning his dressing gown he went down to the kitchen to prepare breakfast, and making a large pot of coffee he poured himself out a cup. Glancing at the clock on the wall he saw they had slept late – it was well past nine o'clock. Stephany entered the kitchen, kissed him lightly on the cheek, sat down and poured herself out a cup of coffee. Taking a slice of the toast he had just made she smiled, and without a blush or look of embarrassment gazed up at him saying, "I love you Arthur", in perfect English. Taking her hands in his he blushed and whispered, "I love you too Stephany, but what does the future hold for us?"

Her remark, "We will see," was cut short by the ringing of the phone in the lounge. Arthur picked up the receiver.

"Mr Hallsworth?" a voice asked.

"Yes, speaking," he answered.

"Simpson, Rowlings and Tansley here. Mr Simpson will see you both at three o'clock tomorrow afternoon, if that is suitable."

"Yes," replied Arthur. "We will travel by train to London and be at the office at the appointed time."

The voice replied, "Good. Was the transport yesterday okay?"

"Splendid, thank Mr Simpson for his kindness."

"I will. See you both at three o'clock tomorrow."

The phone then went dead.

Arthur returned to the kitchen. It was empty so he finished his breakfast, then went up to shower and shave. Stephany was in her room singing one of the native songs in her sweet voice. He dressed and went down to the lounge where he found a pile of letters on the coffee table. Sorting through them, he found that most were bills of which he made a note, as they must be paid without delay. A few were from friends which he was reading when Stephany came in dressed in some more of her new clothes, looking fresh and well rested. He explained that they would be going to London the following day. She sat down and was quietly watching him reading his mail, when they were startled by the ringing of the door bell. Answering it Arthur was confronted by his nephew.

"Welcome Home, uncle Arthur. The solicitors notified us you were on your way home, so we got in some supplies. Hope everything was okay." Walking through the hall and into the lounge he stopped in surprise on seeing Stephany. Arthur made the necessary introductions, saying:

"We have an appointment at three o'clock tomorrow with the solicitors in London."

"Good, tomorrow is my day off so to save you the trouble of arranging transport I will take you up, uncle."

"Thanks, that is most kind of you," Arthur remarked.

"Oh! by the way, a welcome home party is being held in your honour at mum's, due to start at about eight o'clock tonight. See you both there, cheerio," and Clive left.

They spent the day walking round the town, Arthur pointing out various places of interest. After a meal, in a well-known local café, he took her to the park where she appeared to be enjoying every minute. Being a local lad, he stopped to chat with many of the residents; he thought of taking her to the cinema, but dismissed the idea, realising she would not understand the language, although she had a keen intellect and he was surprised at how quickly she was learning English. They returned home in time for tea, afterwards going upstairs to prepare for the party being held at his sister's home where they arrived a little before eight o'clock. Stephany was welcomed with open arms and soon felt and appeared quite at home.

Arthur had to admit she looked lovely in another of her new outfits and everyone there was admiring her; as the evening wore on Arthur was encouraged to relate some of his recent adventures in which all present seemed very interested. They were inundated with wishes of good luck to be the outcome of their visit to London on the morrow. As they were preparing to leave his sister took his arm and drew him aside saying, "That lady is head over heels in love with you."

"What makes you say that?" he asked.

"From the sparkle in her eyes, and the way she looks at you, I hope you are not going to break her heart."

"No sis," he replied. "My feelings are akin to hers, but we cannot make any plans until we see what tomorrow brings, and I know whether she would be prepared to marry and settle down with me in England."

They left for home and, on arrival, decided to go straight to bed, making no pretence this time of having separate rooms. Stephany was in his bed long before him, and when he joined her she held him close in a passionate embrace, gave a deep sigh and, after a lingering kiss, with an arm across his chest fell off to sleep. Watching her lying there beside him he thought, 'She is a lovely woman, and we get on so well together, I trust we can become man and wife.'

Turning off the bedside lamp he soon joined her in sleep. They rose to shower and breakfast early as Clive wanted to be on his way by nine o'clock, in order to take Stephany on a short tour of the city before their appointment, Arthur having promised her a more detailed tour later on. Arriving a little before three o'clock at the solicitors' they were shown straight up to Mr Simpson's office, and after shaking hands with them both he offered each a chair then rang for his secretary who soon appeared, carrying a tray on which was displayed four cups of coffee and a plate of biscuits. Mr Simpson, a mature grey-haired tall slender man, attired in a dark suit, white shirt, and Old Etonian tie, was seated behind his desk, and picking up a blue covered file he checked it. After studying the contents for a short time, he turned to Arthur saying:

"Has the lady brought her identification papers with her?"

"Yes," replied Arthur and, reaching into the briefcase he had set down beside him when he came in the solicitors' office, he handed over a large manila envelope to him saying, "Here they are."

Mr Simpson leaned a little further back in his chair, adjusted his spectacles, looked for a moment at Stephany, then concentrated on the examination of her credentials. Each document was carefully checked: birth certificates, marriage lines of her parents, her passport and identity card, and finally, a letter from Jan Patlovic the mayor of Misakev addressed to the solicitor, which he had handed to Stephany as they were leaving.

He explained that, as a friend of the Kaldev family for many years, he could quite safely confirm that Stephany was the person she claimed to be. Mr Simpson then leaned forward again:

"These all look genuine to me; I regret that I am unable to translate any of it, but we contacted the Embassy of this young lady yesterday, and an interpreter willing to help out is due from there at any moment. Meanwhile perhaps you will relate some of your exciting adventures for us, Mr Hallsworth. You are a most brave and enterprising man to attempt and succeed in such a dangerous quest. Through various channels we have, over the years, tried to trace any living relative of the late Ivor Kaldev, but always came to a dead end."

Arthur briefly explained parts of his adventure to which the solicitor listened with interest, then Arthur remarked:

"Your main difficulty in tracing Ivor's family may have been caused by the constant tribal wars being waged in that part of the country for many years. Life has been very unstable, and there has been little contact with the outside world, but at last the warring factions have decided on a peaceful settlement, and in the future it should catch up with the twentieth. century. We are hoping to return in safety to Misakev once this has all been cleared up."

"Yes, I hope you can," said Mr Simpson. "There must still be a lot of sorting out to be done on Miss Kaldev's behalf. As you say, she has property and her many friends to return to."

They discussed other matters whilst sipping the coffee for a while, then Mr Simpson remarked, "When the interpreter arrives we can continue." A few moments later the intercom buzzed, and he answered it saying, "Send the gentleman in." His secretary entered and ushered in a very smartly dressed young man who spoke in English to Arthur and Mr Simpson, then turned and spoke to Stephany in her own language. When he was seated the solicitor handed him some papers saying:

"They are a transcript in your own language of the papers in this file, which proves to be the last will and testament of the client's brother, one Ivor Kaldev. As I read out each version in English, would you please translate for the benefit of Miss Kaldev? This is the last will of Ivor Kaldev, previously a citizen of Hungary, now a refugee in England. Dated this 21st day of October 1942."

As he proceeded to read through the legal jargon, Arthur watched Stephany and saw a suspicion of tears in her eyes. Mr Simpson paused, and looking from Stephany to Arthur he smiled saying, "We now get to the actual nitty gritty," and continued to read out Ivor's bequests:

> To my nearest living relative, I leave three quarters of my total estate; to my dear friend Arthur Hallsworth, for his kindness to me, and all the work he may have undergone in tracing any of my family, I leave the remainder. If no living relative is found then the whole of my estate goes to the aforesaid Arthur Hallsworth.

He paused again, and looking up from the papers remarked, "I am sure you will be as surprised as I am when I disclose to you the value of the Estate. With the many years of accrued interest, Ivor has left the sum of £180,000 and 85 pence; from this will be deducted our fees and costs, and you Arthur must submit a claim for all expenses incurred; the final figure will then be divided according to the wishes of the deceased Ivor Kaldev. You may now be wondering how a refugee came to be in possession of such a large sum of money; there is no secret and it was not stolen. When he first came to England he was employed as a gardener by Sir William Thomas, a wealthy gentleman. Some time after taking the post he was instrumental in saving the life of Sir William. Bruton Hall was a fine old manor house with extensive stabling out at the rear. Whilst working in the vicinity one morning Ivor saw smoke and flames arising from the stable block. Hearing a cry for help he realised Sir William was trapped inside, and without a moment's hesitation he fought his way into the burning building and brought his employer out safely. Although being a robust eighty-year-old his intensive injuries meant hospital treatment for some considerable time. In spite of having burns on his hands and face, and being overcome by smoke, Ivor made a quick recovery so went back to take charge of the Hall and to keep things ticking over until the return of Sir William, whose only son and heir had been killed at Dunkirk, and as he was the last of his line there was no one to take over the responsibility. However on arriving back at work, he found the army had commandeered the Hall for use as military staff HQ. Ivor paid a visit to his employer, who had now been transferred to a nursing home. He explained that, as he no longer had a job, he had decided to volunteer for service in the British armed forces. Sir William gave him his blessing, wishing him good luck and a safe return. Some two years later, Sir William died, and in gratitude to Ivor for saving his life, he had a will drawn up in his favour. Bruton Hall and its contents, some of which were valuable antiques, were to be sold and the proceeds held in trust for Ivor to claim when the war ended, with one exception: a family heirloom was to be retained, and given to Ivor to be passed down on the female side of his family. A copy of this was sent to Ivor, who when home on leave called on the solicitors, and had drawn up this will of his own. As he did not survive, you are the two who will now benefit. There is still this," and pulling out a drawer at the side of his desk, he offered Stephany a long black leather covered box.

"His will contains a codicil that should his mother or sister be found, this was to be given to the beneficiary of the will."

Chapter Fifteen

Stephany stared at the box for a moment before lifting the lid, when she gave a gasp of surprise. There nestling on a bed of black velvet lay a most magnificent diamond necklace which, when caught by the rays of the sun filtering through the window, caused myriad iridescence to sparkle from the interior. Lifting it from the case she held it up, gazing at it in awe for a moment, then carefully laid the precious article back.

"Is that for me?" she whispered in a trembling voice.

"Yes, and it is very valuable," remarked the solicitor. "I expect it was retained in the hope that it might grace the neck of a charming lady one day, and I can't think of one more charming than you, my dear. I would suggest that it be put into a safe deposit at a bank, or we can keep it here for you, in our vaults."

She nodded and handed it back to him, after hearing the explanation of the interpreter. Excitement from the news of the fortune she had inherited had left her almost speechless; it was all beyond her wildest dreams. When all the legal matters had been completed, and bank accounts with an international bank arranged, they took their leave of the solicitor both still in a daze. When Clive had left them there he had gone to meet a friend, with arrangements made for them all to meet later at a restaurant near Oxford Street.

Arthur hailed a taxi and they were taken to Oxford Street. With an hour to spare he took Stephany on a tour of Selfridges, and a few other large department stores where she gazed in wonder at the display of such beautiful goods. They both resisted the urge to make purchases until certain the money was in their bank accounts. Strolling to the restaurant which was near at hand they arrived at six thirty p.m. to find Clive already there with a table booked.

After an excellent meal, a bottle of champagne was ordered, to celebrate the occasion. Clive was bursting to hear the news, but Arthur waited until the meal ended then poured each a glass of wine and gave a toast to Stephany. Becoming impatient, Clive remarked: "Come on Uncle, tell me all about it."

Arthur smiled.

"You are not going to believe this, but Ivor was a wealthy man. He has left Stephany a fortune making her a rich woman. He also remembered me. I will disclose how all this came about on the way home."

After a most enjoyable evening they left the restaurant and walked to the car park. Stephany got into the car, stretched out on the back seat, and was soon asleep. Arthur sat in the front with his nephew, explaining how Ivor had acquired the money he had left to his sister and himself. Clive was delighted at the news, and on arriving at their destination nearing eleven p.m. dropped them off and resumed his journey home.

After a hot cup of coffee they retired, too excited to do anything more than discuss the day's events, Stephany finding enough English words to express her feelings. They eventually fell asleep, waking refreshed in the morning to indulge in passionate love making. Arthur was the first to bath and dress so went down to cook a good nourishing English breakfast consisting of bacon, egg, sausage, tomatoes and fried bread, followed by toast and marmalade washed down with hot coffee, which they both enjoyed when Stephany joined him later on. The day was spent first conducting necessary business at the bank, then visiting nearby relatives to tell them of their good fortune, and arrange among them for a large party to be held the following Saturday. It took him quite some time after returning home to make her understand what he was planning. He was slowly and patiently explaining, when her face suddenly lit up with pleasure. "Oh! Yes please," she exclaimed. Arthur phoned a good local caterer, who recommended a large hall with the use of a small band. He then decided to phone his circle of friends and relatives who resided too far away to visit, inviting them all to the forthcoming party, and by eight o'clock that night all but two or three had accepted. They decided to spend the next few days quietly at home. Stephany turned out to be a good cook, and soon mastered the use of the gas cooker and various other kitchen utensils. His sister called on Friday afternoon, and the two ladies went out on a secret mission.

Arthur occupied his time mowing the lawns and generally tidying up the garden, all the while musing on his wonderful good luck. Vera and Stephany returned in time for tea; she was loaded with parcels and slipped upstairs with them. Vera left soon after the meal, so they decided to spend the evening watching the TV. Although broadcasting had reached her country she had never watched it, as she knew no one who possessed a set. She found the programmes most interesting, and Arthur thought it might be of help in teaching her English. When the programme had finished, he spent some time trying to explain to her all about the party being held the next evening, then after a coffee they retired.

Vera arrived at ten on Saturday morning to take Stephany to her hairdresser, where she had an appointment for ten thirty. When they had gone, Arthur got out his own car, and went on an errand of his own, making sure he was back well before the two ladies. He prepared a light lunch for them and it was nearly one o'clock when they returned; he could hear them laughing as they got out of the car.

As they entered the kitchen he looked in shocked surprise at Stephany. Gone was the grey from her hair, and the golden blonde shade of her younger years had returned. It was wonderful and had taken at least ten years off her age; he was delighted with the result, and Stephany saw how pleased he was.

They all sat down and enjoyed the lunch. Vera then departed for home to prepare for the evening's festivities. It was a lovely warm day, so Arthur and Stephany sat in the peaceful quiet of the garden prior to having tea, then making their own preparations for the celebration ahead. Stephany was first to take over the bathroom, and she then disappeared into her bedroom giving Arthur the all clear. He was ready and waiting by seven thirty, so decided to engage a taxi for the two-way journey, thus leaving him free to really enjoy the evening. There was no sign of Stephany and the clock was creeping up to 7.45, when she slowly began descending the stairs. Arthur could not take his eyes off the apparition before him, dressed in the height of fashion. She was attired in a beautiful cerise outfit, complete with accessories of shoes and handbag in a shade of light navy blue. A triple string of graduated pearls was round her throat, with a pair of pearl drop earrings dancing from her ears. There was no doubt of her beauty, it took his breath away, and he leaned forward and lightly kissed her on the cheek, not wishing to spoil the lovely make-up. He then walked with her into the kitchen and opening the fridge door he lifted from the shelf a plastic box. He took off the lid to display, nestling in a bed of damp tissue paper, a perfect orchid, the colours of which complemented her stunning outfit. Smelling the perfume, she smiled as Arthur pinned it on her dress; he picked a single carnation from a small vase on the table. Taking it from him Stephany placed it in the lapel of his dress suit. What an attractive and conspicuous couple they were.

It was then the taxi driver gave a blast on his horn so they went out to the car, and were driven to their destination. The hall had been decorated, flowers adorned the tables, and everything was in readiness for the meal. His relatives and close family friends crowded round the couple, admiring Stephany and her outfit, but had difficulty in conversing with her.

They were all asked to be seated, then a delicious first class appetising meal was served. The hall was ringing with lively chatter and banter all round, something of which Stephany seemed quite oblivious; she concentrated mainly on eating and drinking.

Arthur was full of wonder at how she had been transformed from a middle-aged country peasant, working every day in her garden to make a living, to an elegant beautiful woman, looking so much younger than her actual age. The meal over, his brother-in-law rose, saying, "Please charge your glasses. The toast is to Stephany and Arthur and their good fortune."

Everyone rose to drink the toast which Stephany did not seem to quite understand, but her eyes sparkled with pleasure and excitement, as she sensed all were offering their warmest congratulations. Champagne flowed and the talk got louder and the band came on to the podium; tables were cleared and removed to make room for the dancing which soon got underway. Stephany had never danced before but they had to lead with the first dance, and when Arthur placed his arm around her she felt quite comfortable and had no difficulty in following his steps. As many of his friends and relations preferred to chat they sat out for some time, then several of the females claimed him for a dance, whilst some of the men took Stephany on to the floor. She did her best and the men took her mistakes in their stride.

Just after eleven p.m. as the band were making preparations for the Grand Finale, Arthur stepped up onto the platform and, clapping his hands, held them high. Silence reigned. He then beckoned Stephany to join him, and she stood beside him looking bewildered. All eyes were upon them as he took the mike in one hand and placed the other round Stephany's waist. Looking into her eyes he took a deep breath and spoke to her only, saying, "Stephany, my dearest, will you marry me?" She understood and, blushing, flung herself at him, throwing her arms around his neck. "Yes, yes, yes, Oh! Arthur I love you so much."

Releasing himself he took from his pocket a small box lined with white silk and red velvet, in which reposed an eighteen carat gold ring with a half hoop of five diamonds interspersed with three rubies. She gave a gasp of delight as he placed it on her finger. A few seconds later the silence was broken by a crescendo of cheering and clapping, and someone started singing *For he's a jolly Good Fellow*, to which apparently all the assembled company agreed. Everyone seemed most anxious to shake them both by the hand.

When the commotion had settled down they circulated among the guests accepting the good wishes of all around. The midnight hour chimed, and the band struck up with *Aulde Lang Syne*, ending with the national anthem. It was now time for all to return to their homes.

The taxi driver received an ample reward when he dropped the happy couple off at their abode. Tired, but still excited, they were soon in bed where a wonderful day ended in them making love. Their passion spent, they fell into deep refreshing sleep, and had a lie-in the next morning. After a late breakfast they spent a quiet time in the garden where Stephany admired the flowers, filling several vases with the lovely blooms. When they settled down that evening, Arthur, with carefully chosen words so that she could understand, talked about their forthcoming wedding and with mutual consent a date was agreed for late September, which was only three months away.

"A great deal of planning will need to be done as I would like friends from your own country to join us for our special day."

Stephany nodded. "But who will we invite?" she asked, and producing a pen and sheet of paper he made a list.

"First comes the widow Jaunta and her male companion; the priests Father Markovitch and Father Procovitch; Gregor and his wife Lenie, Gerda and her husband Karl, lorry driver Joseph, my Red Cross friend and companion Stanislow Marktov, and the mayor and his wife from your home town of Misakev."

He handed her the list, and after reading it through she remarked, "Very good, but will they have the money to get here?"

"We have the money, and to spare. We can pay the fares and for the accommodation whilst they are here; we must get the invitations sent off tomorrow giving the date and explaining that they will need to provide passports, but that everything else, such as travel expenses, accommodation charges, and any legal queries regarding immigration procedures, will be dealt with at this end, by us. This is all going to take time, so we must get these letters off by airmail immediately."

The following day Vera was informed of the wedding date, knowing that she would soon let the rest of the family know all that need be disclosed until the official invitations went out. As Stephany was a catholic, it would be advisable to visit the local priest and see what could be done regarding the service. Arrangements were made for the wedding to be conducted at the church of St Edward in Kettering, and Father Patrick to be assisted at the ceremony by the Fathers Markovitch and Procovitch, priests from Stephany's native land. Gerda was chosen to be Maid of Honour to her friend and, as the representative of her country, would wear full national costume. Clive agreed to be best man to his Uncle, and the mayor from Stephany's home town was to give the bride away. Arthur's four nieces would be the bridesmaids; Emma and Aimee, the twelve-year-old twins, six-year-old Vicky and four-year-old Ruth. Everything now got underway; caterers were consulted, and the room booked for the reception.

Arthur now decided to keep his promise to Stephany and take her sightseeing before the wedding. Making London the starting point, rooms were booked at the Ritz hotel for a fortnight, with a cruise on the river Thames and a view of the Tower of London, the British Museum, Pall Mall, and Nelson's Column; Buckingham Palace to see the changing of the guard; Westminster Abbey; St Paul's Cathedral, the House of Commons, Big Ben to be seen and heard, visits to Madame Tussauds, the art galleries, plus a passing glance at 10 Baker Street, once home of the famous Sherlock Holmes. A wonderful whole day was spent at Kew Gardens, two evenings were spent at theatrical shows with superb meals afterwards at Claridges.

Stephany began to feel she had been transported into a wonderland.

Their last day was fast approaching and a visit to Cartiers, the jewellers, was now necessary for the wedding rings to be chosen which were to be engraved with the date and initials of each. An order was also placed for the gifts which would be worn by the bridesmaids, all to be sent to their home when ready. Immediately after arriving home, Stephany enrolled at the local college for tuition in English two days a week; she was quick to learn it was not long before she was able to make herself understood, displaying a keen interest in art and English history.

Therefore, Stratford-upon-Avon was next on the list to visit where Stephany was delighted to see the Shakespearean theatre, and spent quite some time viewing Ann Hathaway's lovely cottage and gardens. A few historical places in Lincolnshire also proved of interest; the Boston Stump, with its wealth of history and intricate artistry, plus a view of Burleigh House. On to St Mary's Vaults in Stamford where they enjoyed a superb meal in a real 'olde worlde' setting then on to the fields of Spalding, unfortunately too late in the year to see the beauty of the bulbs in bloom.

A few days later, Arthur decided that some of the places steeped in history in Northamptonshire would be worthy of a visit; Castle Ashby, Boughton House, Fotheringay Castle, the Triangular Lodge designed by Lord Tresham, (whilst languishing in jail accused of involvement in the Guy Fawkes Plot), and later built in the grounds of his estate on his return home to Rushton, the ruins of Kirby Hall (later restored); Queen Eleanor's Cross at Geddington, Rutland Waters and Southwick House at Oundle, where the museum of ancient farm implements completely fascinated Stephany.

With only a month to go now, Vera took Stephany to London to decide on the wedding attire for herself and the four bridal attendants. Measurements were taken, materials chosen for dresses and head dresses and designs agreed upon.

Arrangements then had to be made with the solicitors for the diamond necklace to be sent to Vera's home by security courier in time for Stephany to wear it at her wedding. Light grey morning suits were ordered for the groom, best man and four ushers; white carnations for the gentlemen's lapels, pink carnations for the ladies' corsage were chosen. Vera undertook the duties of supervising dressing the bride and her maids. As the Matron of Honour had no knowledge of a traditional English wedding, her national attire would be a white full sleeved silk blouse, front-laced black velvet waistcoat, and bright red fully gathered ankle length skirt black shoes and stockings.

All activities were now centred around the forthcoming wedding. Although not in the flush of youth, Stephany had not previously been married, so chose a-near-to-bride's traditional colour. She was to be attired in deep cream satin V-necked, short sleeved dress, with tight-fitting bodice, falling in soft gathers from waist to three quarter length hem. A bolero style jacket with long sleeves accompanied, the edges of which, like the entire front of the jacket, would be trimmed with silver sequins, seed pearls and small crystal beads. She was to wear also a matching toque style hat similarly trimmed with eye length veil, white gloves, shoes and stockings, and carry a bouquet of apricot coloured roses, gipsophilia and trailing fern, interspersed with yellow rosebuds. The beautiful diamond necklace would complete her ensemble.

The two small bridesmaids would be wearing high-waisted ankle-length apricot coloured silk dresses with puff sleeves and white lace collarettes, white gloves, shoes and socks, and carry posies of yellow and white rosebuds with fern encircled by golden doilies. The twins would wear identical dresses of bright yellow silk with white accessories, and carry baskets of mixed carnations and fern. The head dresses consisted of all three colours of the rosebuds entwined with stephanotis into coronets, at the back of each a white silk bow with ribbon streamers. A floral corsage was made for Gerda, blending in with her national costume, thus leaving her hands free to take the bride's bouquet. All five attendants would be wearing fine gold chains round their neck, from which the initials of each recipient would be suspended fashioned in olde English capitals in 18 carat gold intertwined and encrusted with seed pearls, gifts from the bride and groom.

The guests from abroad were to arrive five days before the wedding to give them time to locate the hotel, church and the Hall where the reception was to be held. They all seemed slightly mesmerised by the grandeur of the occasion.

The great day eventually arrived clear and bright, the sun making an early appearance. As was customary, the bride had spent the previous night at the home of Vera, in order not to tempt superstition by seeing the groom before their meeting at the altar. When Arthur and the best man arrived at the church it was nearly full, the bridesmaids were waiting outside laughing and chattering excitedly.

Stephany in true style arrived a few minutes late. He turned to watch as she calmly walked toward him down the aisle, but it was not until the ceremony was completed, and she lifted her face to his, that he realised how beautiful she really was. After kissing the bride they went into the vestry to sign the register, and on emerging they walked hand in hand to the strains of *I'll walk beside you, through the world today*.

Stepping outside they found police were in attendance, holding up traffic at the two roundabouts on the main road to allow the bride, groom, and retinue of attendants to pass beneath a floral archway made and held aloft by the friends from abroad, in order to reach a small pretty public garden on the opposite side of the road, where photographers were patiently waiting with various cameras to get some worthwhile pictures. The cameras clicked and a good half hour elapsed before, in a hail of confetti and rice, they were all whisked off to the reception.

A great gasp of surprise went up from everyone at the sight of the five tiered wedding cake, the top one decorated with coloured flags and insignia incorporating the two countries. The centre cake was to be taken back to Misakev by Gregor to share among his customers at the bar and the many market trader friends of Stephany. The party surpassed even the engagement party of three months previously. The happy couple mingled with the guests, being congratulated and receiving many lovely gifts which were handed to Vera and Clive for safe-keeping, until their return from honeymoon.

Farewells were said to the friends from Mirmskov and Misakev, with a promise to visit them all in the near future when they made their return to settle Stephany's affairs.

The time now came for them to bid farewell to all, and go home to change into something more suitable for the journey to Florida, where a month's holiday was to be spent. Stephany felt much more comfortable in her travelling outfit, a pale green two-piece with beige accessories of shoes, gloves and handbag, whilst Arthur settled for light grey slacks, white open-necked shirt, grey-blue pullover and tan shoes.

The long journey was thoroughly enjoyed by both and, having slept some part of the way, they arrived quite refreshed. Having settled into their hotel room, they went down for a meal and a night cap, then retired. Watching his lovely bride undress, and realising that she was now his alone, aroused in Arthur a desire such as he had not felt for years. Lifting her up, he carried her to the bed, where they fully indulged in sharing the love they felt for each other. Stephany was soon asleep, and Arthur lay beside her gazing in wonder at this lovely creature. His thoughts went back over the past months of all he had endured since setting out on his quest. Never at any time had he visualised such a happy ending. Placing his arm around her he held her close and murmured:

"I must be one of the luckiest men alive; all because I eventually got round to keeping the promise made to a dying comrade – *a promise at last fulfilled.*"